Flight of the Soiled Dove

A HISTORICAL FICTION LOVE STORY. BASED ON A TRUE TALE.

MARILYN TOOLE

Contents

Disclaimer   xi

Prologue	1
Telling David	3
Third of July 1876	11
In Love	17
A Dizzying Courtship	19
The Proposal	21
Suspicion	23
The Train	25
Trapped	29
Rage	35
House Rules	37
Breakfast at Noon	41
The Bath	43
The Fever	47
Shorn	49
The Recovery	51
Meeting Lizzie	55
Running the House	59
David	63
A Request	65
And So to Work	67
A Change of Plans	73
The Girls	75
An Opportunity	79
Pennsylvania Christmas	85
Settling In	87
New Challenges	91
The Gypsy	93

Adrift	97
The Gloves	99
Losing Nana	103
Attempted Murder	105
The Visit	107
Meeting Sallie Reed	115
The Plan	119
The Park	121
The Attack	125
The Evidence	127
The Kitten	129
Doctor N. C.	133
The New Girls	135
Caught	139
Moving Upstairs	141
On Edge	143
The Doctor Returns	145
Headed West	147
Denver	149
A Heart Attack	151
The Murder	153
Reprieve	155
Turned Away	157
Together Again	159
After the Parade	161
The Walk Home	163
Rejection	165
The Fog	169
Telling Madame	171
The Move	173
Christmas Eve	177
The Holidays	181
The Escape	185
Admonition	187
The Machine	189

Labor	195
Living Together	197
The Telegram	201
The Funeral	205
The Muff	207
Where s My Daddy?	211
Lunch at the Union League Club	213
Columbian Exposition	217
Coming of Age	219
Hawking Biscuits	225
A Second Visit	229
The Fire	231
The Healthy Man	233
A Warning	235
In the Paper	239
The Explanation	241
After History Class	243
The Bully	245
The Cards	247
The Decision	249
Claire Awakes	251
The Ring	255
I Do	257
Coffee, Black	261
Life in the Country	265
Eastgate	267
Claire Acts Out	271
Meeting Edward	273
The News	277
Rant	279
The Press	283
And Now to Jail	285
Residue	289
The Future	291
Reconciliation	293

Failure	303
Papa Beckons	305
The Mausoleum	309
Claire s Reaction	313
Visiting Matthew	315
The Wren	319
Epilogue	321

Copyright

Heathfield Gardens
Copyright 2023 Marilyn Toole
ISBN: 979-8-9882534-0-2
contact:
HeathfieldGardens27@*gmail*
.com

Dedicated to the Chicago History Museum, the resources of which provided the framework for this era.

Disclaimer

It is not my intent to offend anyone. On the contrary, I hope that depicting the attitudes, prejudices and class distinctions of the period accurately will help everyone recall the deplorable way many folks were treated in the past -as though it were normal. *To forget the past is to repeat it.* I have tried to create the dialogues as I hear them in my head, as though in a movie. No slight is meant by this.

This novel contains scenes of murder, rape, drug use, white slavery, prostitution, crime, abortion, and graft. For this reason all names and certain places have been changed.

The majority of the proceeds from the sale of this novel will be donated to non-profit groups dedicated to halt human trafficking in all its forms.

Acknowledgements

Thank you to my writing teacher and mentor, Virginia Newlin, Ph.D., my editors, Hon. Tolbert Goolsby, also my Chicago history fact-checker Craig Pfannkuche, and Suzanne Bayles for the loan of her Chicago apartment during my research.

And my dear friends and beta readers Tish Calhamer, Mary Wheeler, Brenda Dorrien, Brooke Borden, Ginny Kricun, Ferne Moffson, Harriet Vitale, and the Coquitlam Writers' Group of Vancouver, BC.

MARILYN TOOLE

Prologue

During the nineteenth century, unmarried women had limited options in life. Often born into families unable to support them, they were left to care for elderly relatives. While nursing and teaching were available career paths, both required advanced education. Jobs in factories or shops did not provide sufficient income, leaving few viable choices. Sadly, many innocent young women were lured into prostitution by professional pimps, earning them the title of "soiled doves" by Victorians. Shockingly, it is estimated that approximately ninety-five percent of brothel workers were forced into the trade through white slavery.

Real estate agents were often the purveyors of this illicit lifestyle, buying large houses and hiring madams to run brothels. They then recruited handsome young men to seduce vulnerable girls into faux marriages. For each successful seduction, pimps received a commission.

The world of prostitution had many levels in large cities, ranging from alleyway nickel jobs to luxurious brothels like Martha Webster's in Chicago in the 1870s, charging fifty-dollars an hour.

Sadly, escaping this tawdry life was not easy. Many young women met an early death from drug use, sexual disease, murder, or unsafe abortions. This novel tells the true story of one such girl, based on vital records, news- paper articles, and family stories and letters.

Telling David

That cold but clear fall evening a wind that usually blew off Lake Michigan in Chicago took the night off. Etta twisted her red leather gloves as she paced in her second floor room at the bordello. This evening had dominated her thoughts for the past few days, and she had circled the date on the calendar–October 13, 1877. She expected her lover, David Andrews, at any moment.

She had rehearsed telling him her news but now felt unsettled. Should she tell him at dinner when the bouillon lost its steam or wait until the blue and scarlet flames of the Cherries Jubilee had died down? She decided to trust her instincts. "Tonight will be the night my life changes!" she whispered. "I have followed the gypsy's advice."

Now all she had to do was convince David to follow through with her plan.

Hearing a carriage outside, Etta peered through the heavy curtains to see her lover approaching on the street below. She ran down the stairs to open the door as the bordello was locked to visitors until nine.

A dapper man, one would have noticed David passing on the street—his demeanor, his attire, his carriage—all communicated his high social status in the big mid-western city to the casual observer.

"How's my little dressmaker tonight, Darling! Are you ready?"

"Oh, yes, where are we going?"

"I thought we'd try the Palmer House. It's their beef-steak special tonight."

Special, to be sure, she thought.

They stepped outdoors, where his carriage waited. He helped her onto the cold leather seat and jumped up beside her. She found her usual small talk had suddenly fluttered away and partnered with the chilly atmosphere. She became aware of being uncomfortable around her lover for the first time. Looking at him, she smiled and turned away as the carriage rolled past the dimly lit buildings along West Polk Street.

Her senses seemed sharper than usual. Her ears focused on the sound of the clatter of hooves, the crack of the driver's whip, and the smells of Chicago's filthy streets assaulted her nostrils. The abrupt glow of a globe lit by a lamplighter added to her keen awareness.

She lifted her scented lace handkerchief to her nose to lessen the street odors as she inhaled the heavenly 'Mille Fleurs' perfume David had given her for her last birthday.

Her usual mood, akin to a bubbling spring, had given way to sudden quiet.

"Are you all right, my dear?" David asked with concern.

She glanced at him. "Yes, Love, just feeling a bit under the weather today. A cold has been spreading through the house, and I feel may be coming down with it."

She disliked lying to David but anticipated this night was different.

Down the street, the Palmer House loomed in the moonlight, rising above the city like a dark giant. Tonight would be the first time she and David would dine there together.

David took Etta's gloved hand. He helped her step down, paid the driver, and led her into the elegant hotel.

"Good evening, Mr. Andrews," the doorman said as he greeted the couple.

Because David lived at the hotel with his uncle, the hotel staff knew him well.

"How are you, Alfred?" David said. "Lovely evening, isn't it?"

"Sure is, Mr. Andrews. Please enjoy your evening, sir."

"Thank you," David replied, handing Etta's sealskin coat to the coat check attendant, who gathered the fur in her arms while eying Etta's lush, green velvet, sequined, and beaded gown.

David took her arm. "This way first, Love." Instead of heading for the dining room, David steered her downstairs toward the hotel barbershop. Impatience flooded Etta's mind. She resented any detours to the telling of her great news.

The couple peered in and found the shop open but empty.

"What am I looking at?" asked Etta. "Is this where you have your hair cut?"

"Yes, but I wanted to show you something remarkable. Look at the floor."

Inlaid silver dollars marked the corners of every square foot of marble in the shop. Hundreds of them, shining up and paving the way for ambitious visitors striding across new money.

David and Etta stepped inside and walked carefully across the floor. She thought, in less than three steps, I've covered more than I made in a week working for that tailor in Pittsburgh.

"Oh, my goodness!" she exclaimed. "I've never seen anything like this."

David smiled. "I thought you might appreciate it. Really something, isn't it?"

The pair left the shop and headed up the wide stairs into the elaborate dining room across the hotel lobby. As she entered, Etta gasped as she gazed at the painted cove ceiling, Grecian columns, and towering palms surrounding the tables. Crystal chandeliers winked down at the scene, while a string ensemble played *Moonlight on the Lake*.

A waiter joined them. "Evening, Mr. Andrews; how are you tonight, sir?"

"Just fine, Ben, and you? And how's that new baby?"

"Oh, she doing wonderful, Mr. Andrews—nearly two months now. Thanks so much for asking."

Etta marveled at David's ability to remember the intimate details of the lives of nearly everyone he met. That trait, she guessed, endeared him to his many friends and business acquaintances in the mid-west metropolis. As fifth generation 'old money', he crossed social and racial boundaries without prejudice.

As she looked around the dining room, she noticed only five other guests at table. David liked to dine early as he often had business commitments after supper. On this night, not really wanting to be seen in public with a 'tradesperson', he was aware he was unlikely to run into anyone he knew as most were attending an event.

Etta continued her survey and spotted a friend across the room. She waved at her. "Look, David, there's Louisa—with someone new."

David smiled. "Is that any surprise? She reminds me of Musette in *La Boheme*—gorgeous, flirtatious, and always with a new man."

Etta responded with a slight grin. She knew, unlike the singers who played the role of Musette, Louisa couldn't carry a tune, but she agreed with David—Louisa did get around, all right.

"But I prefer *La Traviata*, you remember," Etta said.

David nodded. "Yes, Dear, I do." He recalled she especially enjoyed the story of the courtesan who had to give up her lover so his sister could marry well. David had introduced her to opera, which she took to like butter on a warm scone.

The couple studied the menu. They chose chilled French champagne, then, from the listed items: Chateaubriand for two, spring peas with fresh mint, and new potatoes.

After ordering, they commenced their small talk.

"What's the latest gossip at the Webster house?" David asked, grinning.

Etta knew David loved hearing the juicy tidbits about the adventures of the 'soiled doves' who worked in the bordello.

"Well, Grace is still in jail—no trial date set yet. Madame told us she is going to plea self-defense."

"I would think she will be successful," David replied, thinking of the poor girl who had stabbed a famous young Chicago resident to death in the bordello little more than a month ago. "After all, think of what he had asked her to do. Any other news?" David asked with a crooked smile.

"Well, you know how strict Madame Webster is about her girls following her rules about proper behavior—Louisa got in trouble for whistling in the house. She thought Madame was out. I'm not surprised, she is such a flibbertigibbet."

They both laughed.

"What was she whistling?" David asked.

"*Jennie, the Flower of Kildare,*" Etta replied. David chuckled.

Etta continued looking around the elegant dining room. Will I be successful tonight, she thought. Will I convince him?

After being served their entrée, the couple ate in silence, the orchestra sounds filling the room.

"Dessert, Darling?" David asked.

"Perhaps, but first, I have something to tell you." The steak stuck in her throat. She took a deep breath and waited until she had his full attention.

"David," she said but stopped before finishing the sentence.

"Yes? What is it? Are you ill?" David looked alarmed.

She giggled. "Well, you might call it that." She paused a moment. "I'm expecting our child."

He stared at her and said nothing. His face froze into a blank expression. She wondered what went through his mind. Did he think she wanted him to pay to get rid of it? Or did he worry she would leave him and move back to Pittsburgh?

"Really," he said, clearing his throat and looking down at his plate holding his partially eaten steak swimming in its red blood.

An eerie silence followed as the restaurant became quiet as a tomb to Etta. No sound came from the orchestra, the bustling staff, or the diners. Time and sound seemed to have stopped. The elegant dining room surrounding them had disappeared as if in a fog.

Now what? she thought. "Yes, I'm due in July." She cleared her throat.

David looked up. "And what are you planning to do about it?"

She froze—a completely unexpected reply. A queasy feeling stirred in her stomach as the chilly October wind returned, rattling the elegant hotel's windows.

David signaled the waiter.

"Yes, sir, Mr. Andrews?"

"May we see the dessert menu? And coffee, please."

He didn't look at her. She felt as though her breath had stopped. His voice seemed to slow and deepen, like a rundown gramophone.

"Henrietta, you know I could never marry you."

Third of July 1876

In another town, at another time, Etta would meet another man, but one socially miles from David. A little over a year before her Palmer House dinner in Chicago, a hot summer sun burned down on Pittsburgh.

Henrietta Ware had toiled five years for R. Straw, Tailor. Every day, twelve hours a day, six days a week, head down, foot pumping, eyes focused on fabrics, she fashioned suits for men she would never see. Black, brown, and navy threads wove the monotonous pattern of her days.

Etta stood about five feet five inches. Curly dark brown hair surrounded her squarish face, the color nearly matching her piercing brown eyes. A straight and strong nose led to a mouth with a determined set that let everyone know not to tangle with her.

She often wondered if she had gotten her eyes from her mother, whom she never knew, as she had abandoned her baby right after Etta's birth, and there were no pictures of her. Her papa never seemed to want to talk about her mother.

That hot day, Etta, engrossed in making buttonholes for a trousers fly, felt a hand on her shoulder. A male worker bent down and whispered something in her ear. She stood and slapped him, nearly knocking him down.

"Leave me alone, you bastard!" she shouted. All the heads in the shop turned. "There she goes again," whispered one girl to her friend. "Another Etta tantrum."

The shop foreman strode into the workroom, headed straight for Etta, who was pretending to concentrate on her work. "Miss WARE!" he shouted. "My office. Now!"

Etta emerged from the office a few minutes later, her face reflecting the contentious meeting. The management had warned that her temper tantrums had gone too far—she bitterly recalled their most recent warning, "One more outburst, and you'll be fired."

The bell jingled for lunch. Etta picked up her wrapped sandwich and headed to a tiny room in the back of the shop.

"Bad day Etta?" her friend Flo asked. Tall, dark, and willowy, with a biting sense of humor, Etta and Flo had first met at the tailor shop. It wasn't long afterward they became roommates at the boarding house that their friendship began.

Etta wrinkled her brow but didn't answer. She unwrapped her sandwich and fanned her face with the brown wrapping paper. "It's so HOT," she complained.

"Well, some of us are talking about going to the Centennial Eve celebration tonight. Want to come?"

Pittsburgh's schedule for the Fourth of July one-hundredth anniversary the next day included rowing, parades, church services, and speeches by government officials.

Etta groaned—she didn't feel like celebrating anything.

Nothing sounded like fun. "It all sounds so boring," she complained. Etta had seen the flyers posted around town. "Those events are all tomorrow, the fourth, here in Pittsburgh. Etta, come on, we're going to Castle Shannon on the train. They're having dancing and fireworks, starting at midnight tonight. Let's go have fun. They are even having a donkey race."

"I think I'll skip that," Etta replied with a harsh laugh.

"Oh, come on, don't be a wet rag. It'll be so much fun, and you might even meet someone." Flo added with a wicked grin.

That comment captured Etta's attention. She relented.

Late that night, after a quick wash at the boarding house, she joined her friends for the encounter that would send her life on a detour she could never have imagined. She donned a blue and white striped dress with wide pleats and lace and added a ribbon to her tawny brown hair. The wind had seized Etta's only summer hat the previous spring. She had watched the ribbons waving goodbye as the bonnet drifted lazily down the Monongahela River towards its destiny downstream with a fallen branch, to be found by a delighted farmer who decorated his new scarecrow with it.

As they boarded the eleven o'clock train, the girls' excitement at being out so late at night was evident to all those around them. The cooler night air caressed their skin and played with their curls as they arrived less than an hour later in the sleepy town of Castle Shannon.

"Listen, I hear the band," shouted Flo. The music, like the Pied Piper, led the giggling girls through the darkness to the town square.

Several couples dotted the wooden dance floor beside the town gazebo which was surrounded by fluttering American flags. Bonfires lit the festive scene. Etta had little trouble finding dance partners. Later, as she sought out a bench for a break and sat listening to the music, she heard someone nearby clear his throat.

She looked around, and there, right behind her, stood the most handsome man she had ever seen. A cigarette dangling from his lip, he leaned against a fence, one leg casually crossed over the other. He looked right at her. Etta, who rarely blushed, felt her face warm and quickly looked away.

"Having a good time?" His voice sounded deep and resonant. He had moved closer to her. She looked up, surprised he had spoken to her.

Etta did not respond and tried to think of something to say. His good looks and steady stare unnerved her. She began twirling her hair, a nervous habit she had entertained all her life.

"Uhh, yes, I suppose."

She looked around for her friends, to no avail.

The man moved towards her, something small and white in his hand. He handed it to her without saying a word, holding her gaze. She hesitated, then took it but didn't look at it.

"Read it," he said. His voice, persuasive, drew her in.

She looked at it, an engraved card printed in a beautiful script. It read,

> 'May I Have the pleasure of seeing you home tonight? If so, keep this card; if not, return it.'

She stood still, trying to sort her thoughts. She had heard about these 'escort cards' gentlemen sometimes gave ladies but had never received one. What a different approach, she thought.

"At least will you let me have a dance?" She nodded.

Etta placed the card in her chatelaine. The handsome stranger took her arm and led her onto the dance floor. Holding her her close, he gave her long looks. Dance after dance, they twirled around the wooden platform.

I could go on like this forever, she thought.

When they stopped for fresh lemonade, he held her at arm's length and looked her straight in the face. "Where are you from, Miss—?" He paused. "Oh, I'm sorry. I don't even know your name—please excuse me. Mine is Billy Black. What is yours?"

She looked down at her hands as she smiled. "I'm Henrietta, but my friends call me Etta, and I'm from Pittsburgh. My friends and I are just here tonight for the festivities. It's a really nice night, isn't it?" She couldn't stop babbling and quietly pinched herself as she crossed her arms.

After exchanging small talk a few minutes, they heard the fireworks begin, Billy took her hand as they seated themselves on the ground and watched the flares blaze in the night sky.

Billy turned and looked longingly at her.

"What?" Etta, embarrassed, laughed.

"I love the way the light plays on your beautiful face," he stated, his gaze not wavering. He leaned over and gently kissed her. A jolt ran through her chest. Etta felt smitten. If not by the charm and physicality of this stranger, then by the attention he gave her. But she was too deafened by bliss to hear that little voice—that gut feeling—that this was too good to be true.

In Love

Etta and her friends spent the rest of the Fourth sleeping. Their lives, pierced by the exhilaration they felt after the night of adventure, were naturally followed by exhaustion.

When Etta awoke late that afternoon, it surprised her to learn that Billy waited for her on the front porch of the boarding house. After dressing, she walked out to join him. "Well, good afternoon!" Billy said with a broad smile as he arose. "How is the lovely lady today?"

He offered Etta his arm. "Would you like to go for a walk?"

My, he does move fast! Etta thought. "Wait, I need to get my parasol. I don't have a hat."

The couple descended the steps and set off for the river. "It's a lovely day," said Etta, a bit confused. The harsh reality of daylight had somewhat diffused the passion of the night before.

Billy looked at her. "You know, Miss Etta, you are even more beautiful in the daylight."

A smile played across Etta's face. Although a popular

dance partner, she seldom knew anyone well enough to say that to her in all her eighteen years. His words felt like a balm to her lonely soul. As the heat of the late afternoon followed the sun on its western journey, they found a shaded spot on the grass by the river to rest. As they sat, a tiny blue sulfur butterfly danced around them. He put his arm around her as he spoke.

Etta did nothing to stop him.

He leaned towards her, whispering, "I haven't been able to get you off my mind," as he toyed with the single curl draped over Etta's shoulder.

Even though the gray-green steel mill tailings and the foul air surrounded them, to Etta, those distractions seemed unimportant with such a handsome man beside her, her hand in his.

Where is this all leading? she wondered.

A Dizzying Courtship

Henrietta had never felt this way. When the tall, handsome Billy swept her off her feet that fourth of July eve, she fell into his arms like ripe tree fruit falling to the ground. She felt relieved to be spared the fate of rotting her life away on the branch of spinsterhood.

"I want lots of children, too," she had once told her papa while visiting him and his brood of five of Etta's half-siblings. She adored babies and always stopped to coo at them as their big eyes stared up at her. She wanted to grab them, hug them, shower them with kisses, tickle them, and make them giggle. She often told her friends she had 'itchy fingers' every time she passed a baby carriage; she wanted to pick the child up so much.

"You should be married, Etta," Flo once told her. "I never knew anyone who wanted a family more than you."

Etta smiled. With the way the relationship was moving with Billy, she felt likely she would become one of those mothers who strolled in the afternoon sunshine while pushing her baby in a carriage.

"What is it that you like about him?" Flo asked her. "Besides that?"

Etta blushed. Yes, Billy seemed uncommonly handsome and charming. She thought he must be at least twenty-five, and she could not believe some coquette had not caught him yet.

"Well," Etta replied, "he's funny, and smart. And he's traveled everywhere."

She didn't mention his seasonal job as a fair worker. She wanted to avoid thinking about the implications of that kind of life for the long-term support of the large family she envisioned.

"He makes me feel . . ." she went on, "safe, loved, cared for. And respected. He hasn't even tried anything funny." She giggled. She and all her girlfriends had known too many of what they called 'handymen'.

"Well, things are looking up for you, Etta," Flo said. "We are so happy for you."

The Proposal

Billy and Etta sat in a cafe enjoying sassafras tea with honey, their knees touching under the table. Between sips, Billy reached over and took her hand.

"Etta, Darling," he paused. "Will you consider sharing my life with me?"

Etta, too shocked to notice the sentence lacked the word 'marriage,' knew they had fallen in love quickly, but his proposal surprised her. She briefly wondered if she would follow him on the fair tour or always sit at home waiting for him.

His deep voice drew her out of her reverie. "Darling?"

Like a bird fleeing a cage, her reply came out before she could stop it. "Yes!"

There. She couldn't reel it back. The words escaped before she could ask him what life together might entail.

Later, at the boarding house, she confided in Flo about the proposal. "What do you think?" Etta asked.

"Why are you asking me?" asked Flo. "It's your life!"

"That's not helpful at all," complained Etta.

"Well, it's your decision. You should be asking yourself what you think, not me."

Etta wondered if she sensed a bit of jealousy in her friend's reply.

She looked down at her hands. Silence had crept in as an intrusive third party-something had just happened to the friendship Etta and her friend shared-something oblique, invisible, but painfully honest.

Suspicion

Flo and a friend poked at the watery porridge at the boarding house.

"Have you heard–Etta's getting married—marrying that fellah she met at the fair, and they're moving to Chicago," Flo told her companion.

"I don't know, it smells funny to me. It's just too fast." The confidant added, "I'm glad she's leaving. I never did like her. Too bossy. I always knew not to get on the wrong side of her."

Billy posted the telegram at the local Western Union office, addressed to 'Mrs. Martha Webster, 544 South Clark Street, Chicago, Illinois.' The wire said,

"GIRL ARRIVING SEPTEMBER 11 NINE THIRTY A M TRAIN STOP PLEASE SEND CHECK STOP."

The Train

Mid-September arrived with little fanfare. Billy promised Etta a beautiful wedding in the rose garden of his mother's home in Chicago. He suggested they could live there until he could find another job. "We'd better leave soon, I hear there's going to be a rail strike." He promised Etta that his mother would meet her at the train station and he would follow in a few days.

He sent her a one-way ticket, a new traveling outfit, and a hat for the trip by special delivery. She smiled as she reflected on his thoughtfulness when the package arrived.

After sending her employer a note of resignation, she gave notice to her landlady, packed her valise, and said goodbye to her friends.

Etta stood on the wooden platform of the station in driving rain. She felt determined not to allow the weather to dampen her excitement, as her heart felt about to implode. She pulled her cloak closer, gloved hands clenching it as though the gesture lent her needed reassurance.

Billy failed to show up at the station to say goodbye.

Has he changed his mind? A knot of anger formed in her chest, and she took a deep breath to settle it.

The train's bellow reached her before she saw it. As it pulled to a stop, the conductor announced its arrival.

"All aboard for CLEEEveland, Fort WAAAAAYne, ChicAAARRgo."

She hesitantly stepped forward and looked around to see what others were doing. It had been five years since she had been on a train, arriving in the Steel City at thirteen when her father had sent her to a foster family after her nana died. She often heard the steel rail giants' roar, lumbering through the darkness under duress, but never imagined she would get to ride on one again leaving Pittsburgh for Chicago.

When the passengers began to board, she picked up her valise and moved toward the steps. Suddenly, someone bumped into her, nearly knocking her down. "Watch out, look where you're going!" she shouted angrily at the young boy running past her. "Imbecile," she muttered under her breath.

The crowd pushed her toward the car door and up the short steps. She wondered what she should do. Where should she sit? She looked into the parlor car and caught her breath at the painted ceiling, stained glass windows, brocade and wicker chairs—even a crystal chandelier. She wondered if she could take a brocade chair. Better not, best take that oversized wicker one. She put down her bag. Only then did she begin to relax. It's happening, she thought. I'm leaving Pittsburgh forever, bound for a glorious new married life in Chicago.

She looked out the window, hoping to see Billy, but saw only an empty platform. The train gave a sudden jerk. She sat back, took a deep breath and sighed.

Worry set in again when the train crossed the Ohio state line. Etta began twirling her hair. Why hadn't Billy been at the station to tell her goodbye? A slight niggle of doubt pushed its way into her thoughts in the form of a memory —the day the two sat on the river bank–a lovely little sulfur blue butterfly dancing around their heads. Suddenly, Billy had lurched forward and clapped his hands, crushing the dainty little creature.

"What have you done!" cried Etta.

"I hate bugs," he replied with a harsh laugh, then grabbed her and gave her a long, passionate kiss.

The chugger-chug of the train assaulted her ears yet somehow soothed her in its rhythm. The fields, woods, cows, and farmhouses flew by, leaving behind eighteen years of a life of feeling as though she never truly belonged. She now anticipated being safe, married, loved, and a mother with her own family.

The train's gentle rocking soon lulled her to sleep. She dreamed of rose gardens, bridesmaids in pastel colors, and soft words whispered under silky sheets.

Trapped

"Chicargo, Chicago, Illinoisse!" The conductor shouted as he walked through the cars of the train.

Etta's heart pounded as she slipped from her seat. The excitement helped her ignore her sore throat and her back, which ached from sitting up all night. Moving toward the exit, she peered through the dirty windows of the passenger car in the hope of seeing the woman who would meet her and become her mother-in-law. Will she like me? Or will she think I am not good enough for her son?

Her mouth felt dry as prairie dust.

She stepped off the train, took a deep breath, and looked around for the older woman searching for her—the girl with the red satin rose. No one seemed to be looking her way. She stopped. What would she do if no one met her? She had no return fare to Pittsburgh, job, or place to stay. Panic had her in its grip. "Stop it, stop it right now," she muttered as she pinched herself. She wanted to appear confident, so she quickly entered the station.

Suddenly a young girl ran up to her, looking at the red rose on Etta's lapel.

"Miss Etta? Henrietta Ware?"

Etta wondered, is this a servant of my future mother-in-law?

"Yes, I'm Etta," she offered. "And you are?"

"I'm Molly. I'm supposed to take you to Madame's house." A tiny thing with a little squeaky voice and a delightful manner, she spoke with a lovely Irish accent. Red curls framed her freckled face. Etta breathed a sigh of relief and smiled.

"Hello! It's nice to meet you." Were you supposed to say that to the help? Etta had no idea what protocol governed the treatment of house servants.

"Come this way, Miss Etta. Our driver is right over there."

Our driver! Thought Etta. My, this is marvelous.

A few minutes later, they pulled up in front of a three-story redstone building on Clark Street in the Levee District of Chicago. The tall, imposing windows across the street winked at the morning sun.

Etta thought, this is even grander than I'd imagined. The driver clambered down and helped her with her bag.

Etta followed Molly into a long, impressive hallway leading to broad stairs. A right turn took them through an ornate parlor—all gilt and velvet, with a thick, rich carpet, an organ, and a glittering crystal chandelier, past the library—to a small office in the rear of the house.

"Wait here, Miss Etta. Madame will be right in."

Madame? Why is she calling her that? Why not Misses? Silence surrounded her. Etta waited.

In a few minutes a tiny woman, not much older than Etta, entered the room.

"Hello, Henrietta, and welcome, We are so glad you are here. I'm Martha Webster." The woman's small, heart-shaped face was surrounded by flat curls. Her hair was black, her eyes dark and piercing. Her voice belied her tiny features.

Webster? Why is her last name different from Billy's? Has she remarried? Etta extended her hand. The woman did not reach out but shook her head.

"No, Dear, you never hold out your hand to someone older than you. You wait for them to hold out their hand to you first." Etta jerked her hand back. Who is this woman, and who does she think she is telling me what to and not to do? A knot of anger roiled in the pit of her stomach. She managed to control her temper for the moment.

"Henrietta, let's get right to it." Martha sat down behind the imposing desk. "You are in a bordello. I run this house, and now you work for me. Billy, who is in our employ, arranged for you to come here. That is not his real name, of course. And now you owe me for your train fare and outfit."

No pleasantries, niceties—just words riding on the edges of sharp-as-knives reality.

Etta felt caught in a dream, and time slowed down. The woman's words dragged out like warm, sticky molasses. Feeling unsteady, she sat back down with a thump. She gulped, which hurt her sore throat even more.

"Wh. . . what did you say?" she faltered.

"You heard correctly. My establishment is the finest 'sporting house' in Chicago. I started this business five years ago, and you are my sixth girl. Our clients are among the most respected men in the city. I expect you to follow all of my rules. No exceptions."

The woman continued, "You will be charged for your

wardrobe, room, and board. Since you will be with the finest clientèle in the city, you need to be prepared to associate properly with these men. You will be charged for your cultural education. Expect extra assignments besides servicing our clients. You begin tomorrow night."

Etta moved forward in her chair as though thinking of bolting towards the door. Madame noticed and paused.

"By the way, if you try to run away, I will have you arrested. The police chief is one of our best customers. And I know you have no money or return fare, so you will end up on the streets, doing nickel jobs in alleyways. So you may as well enjoy your stay with us." With that, Martha abruptly stood up, letting Etta know the interview had ended.

Etta felt breathless. Is this real? Is this happening? Or have I dozed off on the train and am dreaming?

The woman leaned her head back into the office. "And you will call me "Madame, not Mrs. Webster, and certainly not Martha."

Etta stood frozen for a moment. Never, in all her life, had she felt this way. She realized her mouth hung open and slammed it shut.

Molly returned and gestured. "Come this way, Miss Etta," and the pair made their way up the carpeted stairs to the rear of the house. "This is your room."

Etta looked around. The view overlooked an enormous train yard. The roar from the giant behemoths never ceased, and the single dusty window faced a dismal, gray north. Soot from the coal fires and the trains darkened the outdoor window sills. No roses, no beautiful garden here, she thought. Satin and lace embraced the double bed, whose mattress sagged in the middle, witness to any activities.

A large mirror on the opposite wall, hung low enough to reflect any activity on the bed. The painting over the bed displayed a naked woman lying on a chaise with a rose between her legs, gazing languidly at the viewer. A flowered porcelain washstand and pitcher stood silently on a table nearby, awaiting someone to enjoy a quick wash. The furnishings were completed with a wardrobe, coat rack, an ornate maroon easy chair, and an elaborate chaise lounge. Pillows had been tossed throughout the room.

"Your clothes are in here, Miss Etta," said Molly as she opened the wardrobe. Etta peeked inside at the luxurious silks and satins hanging inside. "Breakfast is at noon and is served in the dining room. You can rest now." Molly left. Etta found herself alone, more alone than she had ever felt.

Rage

Etta walked over to the bed and sat down with a plop. She trembled with rage. What just happened? Am I really in a bordello? So far from home? She picked up a quilted decorative pillow and threw it across the room.

She spotted the kerosene lamp. That's it; I'll burn this hellhole to the ground! And then what, a little voice said. Where will you go? Every scenario she envisioned ended with the same question. Where? How?

She lay across the bed, her arm across her forehead. I could write Papa and get him to get me. But shame prevented her from letting him find out what a muttonhead she had been. To be tricked like this! He wouldn't say anything, but she could envision the look, the hurt in his eyes. No, that's not going to work, either. I've got it! I'll become so unpleasant she'll want nothing to do with me, and she'll send me back! I'll fight and scream–hit and bite her clients. That might work! That thought settled her immensely, and she fell sound asleep.

House Rules

Later that morning, Etta found herself back in Madame's office.

"Please sit, Henrietta. I wanted to ensure you completely understand our way of life and rules. Close management on my part minimizes problems with one another, the staff, and our clientèle."

Etta cleared her sore throat. What else, she wondered.

"As I told you earlier, we have the reputation of being the most exclusive sporting house in the city and are listed in *The Gentleman's Guide to Sportsmanship* as such. On the part of my girls, I insist on absolute cleanliness and deportment. That means daily baths–you will be assigned a time every afternoon–absolutely no drinking or swearing, fighting, gossip, sneaking out, or bringing in your own acquaintances."

Again, Etta felt overwhelmed with all the rules but needed to feel better to care. She tugged at her collar, wondering why it had become so warm in the office.

"You will have no boyfriends or lovers. I will assign the

men you will entertain according to my criteria, as you will be trained to specialize in particular pleasures."

She continued, in a dry voice, "You will ensure no pregnancy take place. The girls will show you what to do. If you do get pregnant and choose not to have an abortion, you will leave at the beginning of your fourth month, but you will still be in debt to me and need to honor those charges."

Etta took a deep breath. So much...

Madame went on. "We do want you to stay in touch with your family. I understand you have a father, stepmother, and five half-siblings in southern Pennsylvania."

Etta looked up in surprise. How did she know that?

"Therefore, you will be given a married name and an address where your family can send mail. We don't want them chasing about the country looking for you, and we certainly don't want them coming here, so here is the system we use. You will write to them about your new married life but try to delay any visits they may want to pay you. If they insist on visiting, we will set a meeting up at the house where the mail is sent."

Etta felt relieved by that bit of news. She hadn't had time to think of what she would tell her family in Pennsylvania about her new life in Chicago.

"Any questions?"

"Married?"

"Yes, of course. I'm sure you told your family you were moving to Chicago to marry."

Etta shook her head. She didn't know what to say. It's all happening too fast. She needed time alone to absorb it all and felt physically worse by the minute.

"You have a gown fitting tomorrow at two, as we have a ball coming up. And I've made an appointment for you with our hairdresser." Etta's hair, naturally curly, usually presented a challenge, and she wondered what magic a hairdresser could work.

"You will learn proper table manners and how to speak correctly. I insist on impeccable English and deportment. No loud laughing, waving of arms, or sudden movements; I don't want my girls looking like the other whores here in the Levee District neighborhood. Our house makes several public appearances yearly, such as the annual parade and the First Ward Ball. You will also be attending the theater and concerts, so must make a good impression. Is all of that clear?"

Madame's piercing brown eyes seemed like daggers to Etta. Without question, her demeanor undoubtedly let Etta know who was in charge.

"You may go, and I hope you will do your best here. You are extremely fortunate to have been chosen by our house."

Etta hesitated. "Madame?"

"Yes?"

"What name will I go by?"

"You will be Mrs. King, widow of Mr. Charles King."

"Widow?" she asked.

"Of course. You will tell people who inquire that he died in a carriage accident shortly after your arrival here in Chicago. That will quiet a lot of curious people."

Great, married to a ghost, Etta thought.

Breakfast at Noon

"We must go now, Miss, or you'll miss breakfast," Molly whispered. "Don't take any food 'til you've watched how the others do it."

Etta felt famished. Five girls were seated at the table. Etta nodded at them, waiting for someone to speak.

"Good morning," said one, clothed only in a corset and white cotton bloomers. "My name is Lizzie, from Maryland. Where are you from?"

"Henrietta—you can call me Etta, from Pennsylvania, Pittsburgh." The rest nodded and went on with their eating. Lizzie continued, "This is Louisa, Katie, Grace, and down at the end is Sadie." Etta smiled weakly at each of them, and they nodded to her. She watched how they managed their utensils, drank from the crystal glasses, and signaled Molly for another serving. Etta reached for a roll and a slab of butter with the large dinner knife on her right and slathered it on the bread.

Katie, on her right, elbowed her. "Like this," she whispered. Taking a pat of butter from the butter plate, she placed it on her bread plate, picked up her roll, broke off a small piece, and buttered it. Etta stared at her. Who made these rules?

Etta felt so awkward as she had so many questions. Katie must have read her mind.

"I know you must be curious about so much, but we'll teach you the ways. I think you'll grow to like it here," Katie whispered.

I doubt that, thought Etta.

All business, Madame came in just as they were finishing.

"Henrietta, you may rest the remainder of the day. Grace, you're due for a dress fitting, Sadie; see me in my office."

After breakfast, Etta returned to her room, threw herself on the bed, and fell into a deep but troubled sleep.

The Bath

When Etta awoke, she wondered what to do next, as most people do when they arrive at a new place for an extended visit.

Molly knocked on her door.

"Miss Etta? Time for your bath."

A bath? Etta had never had a bath in her life. She rarely ever had running water.

Molly ushered her down the hall to a large, ornate bathroom. In the center stood a huge tub surrounded by fluffy towels and bottles filled with creamy lotions. Etta undressed and slowly lowered herself into the unfamiliar territory.

The hot water and steam entered her sinuses, her psyche. She felt her apprehension lessen as she luxuriated in the new venue. A faint lavender scent arose, filling her nostrils with its healing aroma. She had never experienced such luxury.

Molly handed her a sponge and a bar of soap. "Now, Miss Etta, here's how we do it here. Lather some soap on the sponge and gently go over your whole body." Her voice lowered, "And pay close attention to your private parts."

Molly looked at the floor as if she were a bit uncomfortable with the nakedness of her charge.

"I'll see you in a bit, ma'am; enjoy your bath." She left Etta to enjoy her watery experience.

When Molly returned with a soft knock, Etta had finished washing.

"Miss Etta, we're not done yet. I'm going to wash your back. Then you have to pat, not rub yourself dry. Remember, we want to keep your skin as soft as possible. And, you see these lotions here?" She gestured towards the marble-topped table alongside the tub. "You choose any one you like and rub it gentle all over. You're going to want to smell nice and feel nice!" She giggled.

Etta nodded. The bathing experience had somewhat dissipated the anxiety she had been feeling.

Etta finished. "My clothes?" she asked the maid.

"Oh, no, Miss Etta, we're finished with those. You'll not need those clothes here. I have a dress for you, and it'll fit just fine."

Molly handed her a gorgeous peach organza frock with lace trim, stockings, and new shoes.

"How did they know my size?" she shot at Molly.

"Oh, goodness, Miss, don't ask me that. I know Madame is wise on these things; she hasn't gone wrong yet."

Etta recalled Billy buying her the new traveling suit. Ah, so that's how it works.

"Don't put your stockings on yet; I've got to buff your feet."

Etta raised her eyebrows and smiled a slight smile. Maybe this isn't going to be so bad after all.

Molly seated her on the chaise and began doing her nails. Etta had heard of manicures but had never thought about the process. She leaned back and sighed. Heavenly. Her stress had evaporated like the steam from the bath.

"You have such tiny hands, Miss Etta," Molly commented as her experienced fingers kneaded Etta's hands. "So, where do you come from?"

"Pittsburgh."

"Pennsylvania?"

"Yes, Molly, I grew up there, but my father lives in southern Pennsylvania with his new family."

"Well, Miss, who raised you?"

"My nana Agnes and my aunt and uncle raised me until I turned thirteen—that's when my nana died. Then my papa sent me to live with a young couple in Pittsburgh."

Molly shook her head. "That must have been so hard."

Etta didn't answer. The file made a whish-whish sound on her clean nails, and Molly's curls bobbed up and down with the rhythm. Etta tilted her head back and reveled in this new pleasure.

Etta yawned—suddenly so sleepy—and the soft bed beckoned. After Molly left, she lay down and drifted into a gentle sleep. Upon awakening an hour later, her throat raged, and she felt feverish. Sitting up and recalling her surroundings and how she had arrived, tears welled in her eyes. She choked back a sob. How could this have happened? One day—fun with my friends, meeting a handsome man, getting engaged, and now–this.

She couldn't imagine a worse fate than having to service strange, hairy men stinking of liquor. A shudder coursed through her body.

The Fever

Molly rapped again. "Lordy, Miss Etta, I nearly forgot! Glad I caught you before you dressed. The doctor's here to examine you."

One surprise after another, Etta thought. Before she could react to this intrusion, a short, wiry, well-dressed man sporting a thin mustache entered. He set his Gladstone black bag on the nightstand.

"Now, Miss Henrietta—is it? I'm Dr. Thorne. Madame wants her girls to be healthy, so I need to examine you if you don't mind."

Etta had an idea of what that entailed. After all, this is a bordello. She felt sick to her stomach.

The doctor, polite and gentle, made innocuous queries about her health background. He began his examination at her head.

He turned her head toward the light of the window and peered closely into her eyes, pulling her lower lids down. "Now, open up," he directed, looked at her throat, then took her temperature and examined her chest and arms, noticing a red rash. He stopped, saying nothing, and exited the room.

Etta could hear the voices in the hall. "I'm afraid your new girl has come down with scarlet fever, Mrs. Webster." Etta couldn't hear Madame's muffled reply—the lull of the murmuring voices sent her gently back to a fevered sleep.

She dreamt of trying to run from a fire, but her legs had turned into tree trunks. A lump of hot coal seared her throat. She couldn't scream or see anyone coming to her aid. Her face burned as hot as teapot steam. She awoke to a rustle and saw a strange woman sitting across the room wearing a white uniform and starched cap.

"Good afternoon, Miss. I'm Nurse Bradley. Mrs. Webster has hired me to tend to you."

Etta didn't answer. It hurt too much to talk. She merely nodded and lay back down. Her fever had soaked the sheets, so the nurse had Molly change them to cool, white, smooth linens, which felt like a lover's caress to Etta's fevered body.

"I have to use the loo," rasped Etta.

The nurse helped her with the bedpan—another indignity. But, too ill to care, she quietly relieved herself.

Shorn

The following days flew by in a blur of treatments. The nurse fed her rennet-whey, rice water, and weak broths and bathed her in Epson salts, ammonia, carbonate, and nitrate silver to counteract the poison from the fever.

Etta's nightmares increased. Relieved to leave the hellish sleep, she welcomed wakefulness with its companions of fever and discomfort. The nursing continued, replaced by a young Irish lass in the evenings. In her delirium, Etta imagined her half-sister, Maryann, had become her nurse.

One windy fall morning, another stranger came into her room carrying a large bag, not filled with physician's tools—but razors, shaving creams, and towels.

"Good morning, Miss," he boomed. "I'm William Boroughs, the barber, and I'm here to shave you."

"Shave me? WHERE?"

He helped her over to the chair. "Just lean back, Miss," he instructed. She heard the clip, clip of his scissors. She jumped.

"Careful, Miss," he exclaimed. "I nearly cut you!"

"What are you doing?"

"I'm to shave your head, Miss."

"You're WHAT?" Etta croaked while staring down at her locks askew on the floor.

"Yes," he replied. "Didn't they tell you? It will help you with the fever. They'll put cold cloths on your bare head, you see, and that'll help bring your fever down."

"No!" shouted Etta. "I will not let you do that."

"Well, Miss," said the barber with a sigh, "Then we're going to have to tie you down," and turned to get the nurse. "WAIT," Etta cried. "Wait." What difference does it make? I'm not going anywhere, and if bald, I could delay the dreaded first night of my new job. "All right. Go ahead," she said reluctantly.

The Recovery

A week later, the doctor reappeared. After a long look at her, he bent down, took her pulse, and asked, "Well, Miss, how are you feeling today? I believe you are looking better."

Etta croaked, "Yes, better, a little." She coughed.

"Oh, I don't like the sound of that!" He said, expressing alarm.

"It hurts to cough."

"I see." He gently pulled her upright and placed his stethoscope on her back. The nurse stood by, quietly watching. A flock of geese quacked their intention of heading south for the winter along invisible celestial paths. Leaves fell from the few nearby trees in their annual death throes. The rail racket outside continued unabated. The room seemed rank and stale, like a long-forgotten place filled with ghosts of secrets.

"Breathe again," spoke the doctor as he moved his stethoscope around. He turned to the nurse.

"Send for Mrs. Webster."

At the knock, Dr. Thorne stepped outside into the gloomy hall. "She is over the fever but I believe now has pneumonia."

Madame flinched. She had hoped to put her new girl to work soon. Every day Etta lay in that bed cost her money, and she wasn't in business for charity.

Etta lay on the damp sheets as dark thoughts invaded her mind. How different all this turned out since her picture of marrying in a rose garden had been shattered by fate. How could she have been so gullible to be taken in by the dashing Billy Black? She felt so grateful that none of her friends or family knew what a terrible destiny she had fallen into.

She felt strong enough to sit up one sunny October day, so she wrote to her father.

Dear Papa,

I apologize for taking so long to write to you. I now live in Chicago, and as you know, I married in September.

My husband Charles was very loving and kind, and we were finding true happiness, but then a horrible thing happened.

A runaway carriage struck him, throwing him into a stone wall.

He died shortly afterward. Of course, I am devastated, but I am determined to make the best of the situation. I have found accommodation with several other lovely ladies. You can write to me at the address on the back of the envelope. Please write soon.

Please tell Anne hello for me and kiss the children.
Love, Etta."

She had never lied to her father, but this letter demanded deception. The truth would shatter him.

Meeting Lizzie

She felt as though she had been in bed for months but could now sit up and become more aware of everything around her.

The bordello sounds caught her ear—footfalls on the stairs–low men's voices, laughter, giggles, groans, the sounds the night makes in secret dark places. Her awareness sharpened daily, and her chest tightened with pain more from fear than inflammation.

Suddenly she realized she had healed enough to leave. But how? She had no money and no place to go. Madame had told her she would send the police after her if she tried to escape. The local jail certainly wouldn't be as luxurious as her room at the bordello.

Now only her fast-growing hair stood between her and the men she would be servicing. She began to snip off short pieces of it to hold onto her safety net a bit longer. Then she realized Madame would notice and might have privileges taken from her–her meals were still being delivered to her room.

One Sunday, she heard a little rap on her door, and the handle turned.

"Etta? May I come in?"

One of the bordello girls entered. She hadn't seen any of them since that first day and barely remembered her.

"Hi, I'm Lizzie. I thought you might like some company."

Etta quickly reached for a scarf to hide her baldness.

"Oh, don't worry about that. I'm used to it. It'll grow back."

Etta smiled. She appreciated the kind words.

Lizzie, a rather short, chunky brunette with kind eyes and thick lashes, approached the chaise. "May I sit down?"

"Of course," replied a delighted Etta.

"So, how are you feeling? You gave us all quite a fright," Lizzie asked, her brow furrowing.

"Better, thank you. Did anyone else become ill?"

"No, Madame truly stays ahead of these things and got you help immediately. You are fortunate. So many people die from it." She then turned quickly away, realizing she may have said something insensitive. "Sorry. I shouldn't have said that."

Etta smiled. "That's all right. Don't fuss about it."

The pair continued with small talk when Etta said, "Do you mind if I ask? How long have you been here?" Etta wondered if her own journey to the brothel had been unusual.

"A couple of years now, but I'd been in the business for a while. I came from Maryland and worked for another madame up the street, but the 'Good Ladies of the Baptist Church' talked me into leaving. They were picketing in front of our house every day and convinced me I would be better off out of the 'Life.' The living arrangements made by the ladies were adequate, but my pay at Marshall Field's was dreadful, so after a few weeks, I left and came to work here. I'm much better off now--I'm so glad I returned."

The shock rang through Etta. She's glad she's returned to the 'Life?', The one I dread so much.

"And Madame? What do you know about her?" Etta ventured, hesitant to ask the question.

"I heard she was from Boston, that her father, a surgeon, died when Madame was in her teens."

Lizzie walked to the window, gazing at the filthy alley and tracks below. Another train roared by, drowning out her words.

"What did you say?"

Lizzie continued. "Someone told me she married young, but her husband died soon after under mysterious circumstances. An inquest followed, as the death appeared suspicious, but no charges were filed, and Madame inherited a small fortune." She turned back to Etta with a grin. "Do you think she did him in?"

Etta shook her head; How would I know?

"So how did she end up here in the mid-west?"

"I heard she was looking for a good investment, so followed the crowds to Chicago after the big fire of 1872. Lots of opportunities here, then; Phoenix, rising from the ashes." She paused. "Those ashes have lined a lot of pockets." She sat back down and fell silent, looking at her hands.

"What, what are you thinking?"

"Just how different my life would be if all those things hadn't happened. Sometimes, I wonder if our lives are just threads in a tapestry, woven by some unseen being, never to be told what our whole picture looks like."

Another train roared by but escaped the girls' notice, so utterly lost in their thoughts as they were.

The supper bell rang and Lizzie stood.

"Please do stop by again. I hadn't realized how much I have been missing company."

"I will, for sure," Lizzie replied and left for supper.

Etta lay back and thought about how much she liked this girl. Puzzled why she didn't regret returning to the Life, she wondered, can I learn to live with what I will be doing?

Running the House

A few days later, Lizzie revisited Etta. Her recovery brought so many questions to her mind.

"Lizzie, I hope you don't mind me asking, but..."

"That's all right; I know you are wondering, about life here." Lizzie laughed. "Well, I'll start at the beginning. We open at nine when I put the wooden sign with a red rose 'open' sign out. Madame's appointment book is usually filled every night. The clients are admitted by Arthur, the butler, given a glass of champagne and a cigar, then greeted by Madame. She decides which girl each guest will visit, according to their preferences."

She rose and began pacing around the room, looking at the floor, "The men discreetly place cash—in an envelope with their name on it—in an ornate box in the parlor. Madame checks those before the clients are ushered upstairs by Arthur. She doesn't miss a trick, believe me. If someone looks not right to her, she'll send them away to get a certificate from the doctor. Or tell them no one is available." She paused. "Any questions?"

Etta struggled to get the words out. They were sticking to her teeth like taffy. "Um. . . uh."

"What? What is it?"

Etta struggled again. "How–how do we prevent a . . . a . . ."

"Pregnancy?"

Etta nodded.

"We use sponges and douche afterward. If we get pregnant, we have to either leave the house or get rid of it with tansy leaf tea; a difficult decision for some." She sat down and lit a cigarillo. Etta sat upright, as she'd never seen a woman smoke.

Lizzie went on, "That's how it goes til four a. m.—that's when we lock the door and retire. That's it."

"So, what do you do all day?"

"Well, breakfast is at noon, as you know, we have lessons all afternoon 'til four–then we're free til supper."

"Lessons in what?" Etta's imagination had taken off.

"We learn etiquette, proper grammar, carriage, news, and world affairs, things like that, you know, so we can talk to the men."

"Talk? You talk?"

"Oh, yes, sometimes that's all they want to do. You'd be surprised how lonely some of these clients can be."

Etta fell silent. She'd never thought about providing companionship. Hmmm, she thought. Fascinating. And surprising.

"So we don't know who will be with us until they show up at our room?"

Lizzie nodded. "That's right, Etta. Surprise! Of course, if a client likes you, he'll become your regular. I have a couple of regulars," she went on, "which can make the job easier, so be sure to make a good first impression."

Etta felt her plan to be as disagreeable as possible to her clients fly right out the window. "Oh, drat!" she whispered to herself. "that will not work."

Lizzie took a long drag off her cigarillo, blowing the smoke toward the ceiling.

The smell does mask the stench from outside, Etta thought. I should take it up.

"And..." Etta hesitated. "What if they want you to—you know."

Lizzie laughed. "Well, at fifty dollars an hour. . ."

Etta interrupted. "Fifty dollars an hour? That's more than two and a half months' pay for a normal worker!" She sputtered–"that's–that's–350 dollars a night for each girl times five means she takes in nearly 2,000 dollars every night."

"I know, unbelievable, isn't it? There's so much money flying around these days, especially since the fire of '71. Anyway, at that price, some of them do get particular. But don't worry. It's just all part of the job. All you have to do is act like you are enjoying it if you know what I mean. As they used to say, 'just close your eyes and think of England'." The girls laughed. They'd both heard that nugget of Victorian advice regarding sex.

"Then, when you've been here a while, you may be given extra assignments— you know, after she gets to know you better."

"Like what?"

Lizzie peered around the door to the hall, then closed it. Her voice dropped.

"Louisa, for instance, knows her way around Chicago politics—her dad was active in the Republican Party when Lincoln got shot—so she tries to pry that kind of information from her clients. Madame always has to be aware of which way the political wind is blowing to protect her business interests," she added primly. "Louisa has been known to change a political belief or two while with someone between the sheets," she giggled.

How clever. Etta began to cough. The spasms seized her frail body.

"Oh, I'm so sorry I'll put it out—I wasn't thinking." Lizzie looked around to find a place to put out her cigarillo.

The smoke hung in the air like an insult. "Are you all right?" Lizzie rose to get her a glass of water.

"Yes, please go on."

"Grace is good at getting local gossip out of the men—tidbits that could further Madame's hold on the local clientèle. Rumor had it that she often does resort to blackmail to keep her customers in tow." She added in a pleading tone, "don't tell anyone I said that."

David

Concerned about a pending real estate deal, David Andrews paced back and forth in his Palmer House Hotel suite overlooking Lake Michigan. The loose ends were nagging at him. He stopped and stared out the window. The lake glittered as if carelessly scattered diamonds had been tossed onto the waves.

His uncle Matthew walked in. "Well, hello, Son." Matthew always called his nephew' Son,' as he had been like a father to David and his older brother, Will when their mother died of child-bed fever at David's birth.

"Is something the matter? You look worried."

David explained the troubling parts of the deal. Also in real estate, Matthew expertly navigated him through possible solutions, and the men sent downstairs for supper.

Over cold consomme', raw oysters, and Kentucky bourbon, Matthew brought up a possible lot for sale that might interest David. The property lay in Hyde Park, ripe for development.

"A Mrs. Martha Webster owns the property," Matthew said. "Are you familiar with the name?"

"Of course," replied David. Everyone knew of the infamous madame who ran the most exclusive bordello in the city.

"You may want to drop her a note if interested."

"I will, Uncle. Thanks so much for the tip."

David didn't know it, but with that decision his planetary orb had just shifted.

A Request

David penned a note to Mrs. Webster expressing his interest in the property she had for sale. A few days later, he quickly slit open her reply with his sterling silver letter opener.

"Dear Mr. Andrews,

I noted with some interest your letter of last week. I would like very much to discuss this potential transaction with you.

Kindly meet me at my office at the below address at ten in the morning Tuesday next.

Very Truly Yours,
Martha Webster"

David looked at the address. Of course, it's in the Levee District, he thought. It could have been called 'Chicago's Sewer' for all the vice in the neighborhood. It was common knowledge that most of the bordellos and bars harbored criminal deals in that neighborhood. Attempts by the WCTU, the Baptist Church, and various other well-intended organizations to clean up the neighborhood failed. The nefarious goings-on were too entrenched with the city politics of the day for the well-intended groups to have any effect.

He leaned forward at his desk, elbow on knee, and gazed outdoors at the wind dancing a frenzied Tarantella with the city. This meeting could be a risky move for me. Being seen at a bordello could start a wildfire of gossip in Chicago's polite society. All the Andrews men were listed in the *Social Register* and belonged to the city's most exclusive men's clubs. No society man wanted to be a recipient of the dreaded 'black ball' of rejection from any of their hard-won memberships due to a scandalous rumor. Many elite Chicago families looked the other way when their sons visited the bordellos, which seemed more appropriate than an unwelcome pregnancy. A southern family, David's family were staunch followers of the Baptist Church. The faithful looked down on such tawdry practices among its brethren.

David arose and began pacing again, weighing the advantages and disadvantages of such a visit. The sale would be fine, so David's acute business sense won out, and he set out for the bordello the following Tuesday morning.

He stepped down from the carriage at the address, looked right and left, and strode the few steps to the entrance.

And So to Work

Etta finally felt well enough to begin work on her back, but the familiar dread overcame her.

One afternoon Madame Webster visited. "Well, how do you feel," she asked as she sat on the edge of the bed.

"Better, thank you, ma'am," an emaciated Etta replied. She now weighed just over 100 pounds.

"I think it's time for you to be earning your keep, young lady. Your illness has cost me a pretty penny, you know."

Etta nodded. "But what about my hair?" she asked, touching her bald head and hoping for a further delay into the quickly approaching dark world.

Madame reached into a pocket and pulled out a long scarf. "Sit back, dear—I'll show you how to wrap this. You can wear it any time you are going to be seen."

She wound the long turban around Etta's head, tucking it in at the back.

"You can even add a brooch if you like," said Madame, stepping back to admire her handiwork. "Any questions?"

"No, ma'am," gulped Etta. The day finally arrived.

During her illness, she had thanked whatever guardian angel watched over her, but today it seemed her luck had run out.

Molly rapped softly and opened the door. "Excuse me, Madame, a Mr. Andrews has arrived."

"Oh, my, I nearly forgot. Please show him to my office, Molly, thank you."

Nearly dressed, Etta heard another rap on the door a few minutes later. "Yes?"

"Molly, here again, Miss Etta. Madame would like to see you in her office."

Now what? Upset enough without being called on the carpet again and still weak, she slowly descended the stairs, holding the railing with both hands so as to not lose her balance.

Upon seeing a man in her employer's office, Etta quickly turned away and put her hand on her turban.

"Mr. Andrews is one of my business associates. Mrs. King, may I present Mister David Andrews." Etta nodded, and David stood and bowed.

"At your service, Ma'am," he said with a lovely Virginia accent and a smile to match.

Madame said, "Etta, I hate imposing on you again, but I have a favor to ask of you."

Etta looked up. What could this be? Is this man to be my first client? Why are we meeting in Madame's office? In the middle of the morning?

"You worked for a tailor in Pittsburgh, am I correct? For several years? At least, that is what I heard."

Etta nodded.

"Mr. Andrews had a mishap in front of our house, and his trouser cuff was badly torn. I wonder if I could presume upon your sewing talents to repair it?"

Etta bent down, holding her turban, and looked at the cuff. "Yes. I believe I can mend that."

The pair followed Madame down the back stairs to a large basement room with half-windows looking out at the feet of passers-by on Clark Street. The windows faced west, so offered abundant light. A large table sat below the windows with a Singer treadle sewing machine at one end. Against the wall were laid several bolts of stunning fabrics–silks, satins, taffetas, and linens. A tall floral screen stood in the corner, with a dress form and a small chair nearby. On a narrow shelf on the other side of the room sat rolls of laces and other trimmings. Hundreds of spools of colored threads hung on a peg board like a rainbow. Etta gasped. She had never seen such a well-outfitted sewing room.

"I'll leave you two now," said Madame as she turned and headed back up the stairs.

Etta cleared her throat and turned to look at David. He stood around five-eleven, a tad stocky but with a gentle demeanor that belied his build. His dark gray suit, vest, and highly polished shoes—which looked like they had never met a scuff—radiated money and class. He wore a snowy white shirt, as smooth as a newborn's bottom. A stunning black pearl held the cravat he sported in place. His hands looked as though they had never brushed against hard work. His manner showed breeding and education. She had never been this close to such a gentleman.

Etta realized she had been staring and caught herself. "What happened, Mr. Andrews?"

He leaned and pointed to his left pants cuff. "As you can see, my cuff got into a tussle with an extremely ill-tempered cur outside your establishment. The cuff lost."

Etta laughed. She liked the way he put things. "Please," she said, pointing to the screen for him to disrobe.

Following her lead, he stepped behind the screen and removed his pants. His arm came out from behind the screen holding them. She tried not to look but did notice his silk stockings and shoes. Her eyes widened. His shoelaces look as though someone had ironed them!

She picked a dark gray spool, sat at the sewing table, and began her repairs. David peeked out from behind the screen so he could watch her. She didn't notice, as her preoccupation with her assignment commanded her full attention.

David immediately found himself smitten with her appearance, manner, and beauty, even with the turban. But he did notice a sadness in her eyes and wondered what had placed it there. She is married–how did she end up in a place like this, he asked himself. His heart ached with compassion. He wanted to take care of her—to hold, soothe, and murmur soft reassurances into her tiny ear. Etta's voice jerked him out of his reverie. He caught himself. You cannot become interested in this girl, his conscience whispered.

"Here you are, Mr. Andrews. You may want to look at the repair before you put them on." She tossed his trousers over the screen.

David examined the cuff. He could barely find the repair. What a fantastic job she has done. David had only one primary skill–that of sales—and admired the talents of others and the diligence it took them to excel at their jobs.

After dressing, he stepped out from behind the screen and reached into his pocket for his wallet. He pulled out a five-dollar bill. "Very nice, young lady!" David said enthusiastically.

"Oh, no, Mr. Andrews, I couldn't." cried Etta. That amount surpassed the money she made in a week at the tailor.

"No, please, Miss, I've already paid Mrs. Webster for your work—this is just a little extra thank-you for a nice job."

Etta shook her head.

"Please, Miss, take it. I like rewarding a job well done, and you deserve this. It can be our little secret," he said with a twinkle in his eye.

Etta demurred, and the couple headed back up the stairs.

David floated back to his hotel along the dirty sidewalks. No doubt!—despite the social bonds placed upon him and the constraints of his upbringing, he had finally met her—the one.

A Change of Plans

After breakfast the following day, Etta again found herself summoned to Madame's office.

"Henrietta, please sit down."

Not again, she thought.

"I've called you here to tell you that I have had a change of mind about you. Even though you are quite attractive, I have given it a great deal of thought and have decided that I need your talent and experience more as a dressmaker than as an upstairs working girl in my establishment. Sadly, I just lost my former dressmaker due to old age and arthritis. If you accept, your evenings will be free to do whatever you like."

Does that mean I don't have to be with men? Etta thought but hesitated to say it out loud.

As if she read her mind, Madame added, "As long as you remain in this position, you will not be required to attend to our clients. Is that acceptable to you?"

Etta inwardly giggled at the language Madame used in describing her 'establishment' and her 'clients,' as though words alone could elevate the reputation of the bordello to that of a great museum.

"Yes, Ma'am, that would please me." She wanted to jump for joy and dance around the room but wisely sat quietly and nodded, not looking up for fear Madame would note the unparalleled pleasure on her face.

"Of course, I will have to move your living quarters. I will set up a cot and washstand for you down in the sewing room. However, you may mingle with the girls—including meals—and use the main bathroom and tub as much as you like. I think you will enjoy it here."

The Girls

As the warm fall days yielded to winter, Etta got to know the girls at the bordello. She found plenty of time to chat when she fitted their beautiful gowns to them. Each girl had her own unique story of how she ended up working on her back at Madame Webster's facility.

Grace came down one morning to have a dress repaired. She had a rousing time at a recent ball and had torn her gown.

"Can you fix this?" she wailed to Etta. "It's my favorite dress. I'm afraid I got a bit carried away!"

Etta examined the exquisite blue brocade garment, turning it over carefully. She wondered what could have happened to cause such a tear but knew not to press the issue.

Grace, nineteen, a voluptuous blond with a button nose and a slight lisp, had a rowdy laugh. Her chatter sometimes drove her companions crazy, but they liked her despite it.

As Etta mended, Grace waited, sitting on the tiny chair

nearby. She wriggled her foot as she spoke. "Where are you from, Etta?"

"Pittsburgh, Pennsylvania."

"Oh, yeah, I forgot. Do you have family there?"

Etta removed the pins from her mouth. "Well, sort of. My nana, who died when I was thirteen, raised me, so my papa sent me to live with a family in the city. After a year at school, I went to work for a tailor."

"And your parents?"

Etta hesitated. She felt ashamed that her parents never married and her mother had abandoned her when baby Etta was only a week old. "My father married and has five children," she replied. "We are very close."

"Does he know where you work?"

My, this is a nosy one! "I told him my husband died in a carriage accident and I work as a dressmaker." All the girls were familiar with the carriage accident story. Etta quickly switched the subject.

"And how about you, Grace, where are you from?"

"I'm from Sandwich, northwest of here. I came to the city to find work but couldn't manage on factory wages—so I decided to join the bordello."

She said it matter-of-factly, as though discussing where to add a pleat on her gown. "I've never regretted my decision," she added as she twisted in her chair, looking over Etta's head at the feet passing by outside the window. "I have money, steady work, a beautiful place to live, friends, and an active social life. What more could a girl want?" She smiled a toothy grin at Etta.

Etta couldn't imagine Grace's living the 'Life' but said nothing. To her, none of those benefits would have been worth it to have to bed strange men.

. . .

Sadie, tall, lean, and no-nonsense with long coal-black hair, hailed from Iowa and was debauched by a man who met her in a Bible study class. Mark seemed out of place in the little class of eager students. He told Sadie he wanted to start a Christian youth group in Chicago and needed an assistant. He could even provide a place for her to live. By the way, could she type? The lure of the big city and the salary he offered were tempting, and she quickly said 'yes'. He put her on the train at Des Moines and gave her a red rose to wear so his associate would recognize her at the station. Sadie was twenty.

Etta learned all this over a long session with Sadie while choosing a fabric for her winter ball gown.

Katie, twenty-five and from Tennessee, was easily recognized by her heavy southern accent. Thick eyelashes framed her hazel eyes, as big as her large family. Her black hair sported a distinct widow's peak, and she had a tiny mole on her right cheek, which gave her an exotic look. She was clerking in a candy shop in Clarksville when a stranger entered and began a conversation. He smiled.

"Hi, I'm Abner, from Chicago, and I was looking for work in the area." A jelly bean addict with bad teeth, he became a regular store customer, and Katie found her heart quickening when she spotted him entering the shop.

"We have an opening for some help at the store," she told him a few days later. "Might you be interested?"

He jumped at the chance and began his duties behind the counter.

After a few weeks, he told her he had fallen in love with her and proposed. Katie, a girl who had always wanted to live in a big city, said 'yes' quickly, especially after he told her they might do better with a shop of their own in Chicago. The physical attraction between the two steamed up as quickly as a hot August afternoon.

"You know what, Katie?" he asked one day as his chin snuggled her long willowy neck. "I know someone who can marry us right away. How about we get married this Saturday?"

"Saturday?" Katie's astonishment was clear. "Isn't that rather soon?"

He grabbed her and pulled her close. "I can't wait!" he whispered.

The pair stood in the town gazebo while the 'preacher' married them. They kissed and spent a heavenly wedding night in a cheap hotel in Nashville.

The next day, the pair traveled to the train station. On the platform, Abner told her, "Katie, I have a few things to tidy up before joining you, so I want you to go ahead. I'll be there in a day or two."

"Oh, no." She exclaimed. She didn't want to go on without him and stepped down from the train.

"No, sweet thing, I insist." He touched her shoulder and gently pushed her back towards the train steps. "You go ahead and get our house ready for us. My sister will meet you at the station. Be sure to wear this red rose in your lapel so she will know you." He kissed her and disappeared before she could object any further.

She never saw him again. She later found out the marriage wasn't legal and that the 'preacher' and the 'ceremony' were shams.

An Opportunity

Few eligible young Chicago socialites enjoyed David Andrews' company. He received many invitations to call, but business always came first, and, when with a lady, his mind usually wandered elsewhere, making him a rather dull companion. But this was different. She must be a widow–working in that place–could this be–love? He shook his head. David knew polite society in Chicago would not allow him to court this 'trades-person,' but love can often surpass social barriers.

Helpless, he couldn't get the dressmaker out of his mind. Whether signing a bill of sale, riding in a brougham, or enjoying a scoop of pâté de foie gras, his mind insistently pulled him back to that short visit to the girl at the bordello. He found himself in a tug of war his growing feelings for her and his conservative conscience.

One late fall day, while the wind re-arranged everything not tied down in the city, David and Uncle Matthew were lunching at the Chicago Club.

"Uncle, what is that on your vest pocket?" David asked, leaning over his cold melon soup.

"What?" Matthew looked down but couldn't see the problem. David leaned closer. "Here. Your pocket has a tear."

"Oh, no!" said Matthew. "This is my favorite vest." A moment passed.

"I have found someone who does amazing work." David offered, trying not to show his excitement at perhaps seeing the little dressmaker again.

"Give me the address—I'll send it by courier," Matthew said.

David wrote it down, but after Uncle finished wrapping the vest in brown paper and string, David didn't give it to a courier. He kept it to deliver himself and sent a note to Mrs. Webster requesting a meeting.

David smiled when he received a reply a few days later.

"Dear Mr. Andrews,

I received your request in the late evening mail. Of course, you may visit again. As you know, we have a real estate business to complete, so please come Wednesday next at ten.

Yours very truly,
Mrs. Martha Webster"

The following Wednesday, promptly at ten a. m., David once again stood at the door of the bordello. His heart beat faster this time. He looked around and saw no dog tearing at him, as happened the last time he stood at this spot.

Arthur ushered him into Madame's office. "Good morning, Mr. Andrews."

"Good morning, Mrs. Webster; how have you been?"

"Well, thank you. Business is excellent at this time of

year—approaching the holidays—and I am pleased to finalize the sale of the property we have been discussing."

David signed the papers and, clearing his throat, said, "Madame, I hate to bother you again, but your little dressmaker did such a fine job on my pants cuff that I took the liberty of bringing another little mending task for her. I hope you don't mind this imposition."

Not pleased, Madame thought, he's here, and it shouldn't take long—he could possibly bring in more clients to the brothel, so she acquiesced.

Madame led David down the back staircase. His heart pounded harder. What is the matter with me?

Etta was seated at the treadle when he entered. She had lit a kerosene lamp to improve the dim winter light. She looked up, her face softly lit by the warm glow.

"Mr. Andrews!" She smiled broadly. "What a surprise! Has a cur found your other pants leg?"

Her humor enchanted David. He laughed and suddenly felt self-conscious.

"My uncle, with whom I reside, has torn his vest pocket, and . . ."

Suddenly, David found himself at a loss for words. He looked at her and noticed her hair had grown slightly, revealing a gentle wave. She looked beautiful. She had added a bit more weight which rounded out her young body nicely.

"Mr. Andrews? Are you all right?"

David cleared his throat. He couldn't believe what being near this woman did to him.

"Ah, yes, Miss, as I was saying," he continued.

"Let me see." She moved close to him to examine the package. Just inches from him, he caught her scent and inhaled sharply.

"Ah, yes, just a small tear. I can repair it while you wait. Please, have a seat," and she motioned to the nearby chair. Etta took the vest, picked out a brown thread, and sat at the table to mend it.

David now had time to study his new love interest—flawless pale skin, deep brown eyes, an excellent straight, narrow nose, and pixie lips. His gaze moved down. He liked what he saw, even with her dress and apron covering most of her body.

He caught himself and sat up straight.

"Where are you from, Mrs. King?"

"Pittsburgh, sir."

"And you were employed by a tailor?"

"Yes, sir."

"Please, call me David."

Etta looked up. Where is this going? Is this more than a business call? A little bell tinkled softly in the back of her mind.

She bent down to her mending. Before David could query her more, she handed him the vest. "There, done."

David found himself wishing the pocket tear had been worse. This visit needs to be longer, he thought.

"Oh, it looks just fine. My uncle will be pleased." How to extend the time with her? "Miss, I've been thinking and would like you to make a suit for me. Would you consider taking that on if it is acceptable to your employer?"

Etta thought about it. She looked around the shop at the stunning fabrics and notions she loved. She thought, I dread working with those dull tweeds and serges, but I would like to see this man again. There was something about him—she couldn't put her finger on it, but she felt such a strong attraction to him and sensed he felt the same.

She liked his appearance, not only his dapper attire but his physical appeal. David had a squarish face with slightly wavy hair parted in the middle. The top of his head looked relatively flat. A long narrow nose led up to eyebrows that began bushy but seemed to forget where they were headed. His deep brown eyes held a sparkle as though he had just thought of something amusing.

"Yes, sir, I believe that would be acceptable."

"Very well, then, I'll speak to Mrs. Webster." David turned to leave. "Oh," he reached into his pocket again.

"Oh, no, Mr. Andrews, I couldn't!" Etta objected.

David gave her a broad smile. "I insist."

After he left, Etta realized that if she did take on this new task, she would have to fit him, a job usually done for men by male tailors. She closed her eyes and tried to recall if his crotch needed to be tailored to the left or the right, but she had been too busy mending to notice. How am I going to manage this? she wondered. Ah! I'll have him bring an old suit; I can use that as a pattern—no need to re-measure him.

Pennsylvania Christmas

Etta now had ten dollars in a little box hidden in the notions drawer. She seated herself at the table and wrote her Christmas list: 'Papa: pipe and tobacco; Anne: small handbag and embroidered hankie'.

She sat back, pen still in hand, as her mind drifted back to past Christmases with her father and his family in Pennsylvania, with the gently falling snow outdoors and the pumpkin smell permeating the house. She closed her eyes.

* * *

Etta h a d always b e e n grateful her father invited her to spend Christmas with him every year since he married that Scottish lady, Anne. Etta had traveled thirty miles from her host family in Pittsburgh to his house in Freeport every year as a child.

The long, cold trip by wagon seemed worth it to her, as, once a year, she felt so loved. Her happiest days were when she felt part of a family, with a real father and—albeit half—brothers and sisters. She adored them and, when with them, felt complete, whole, something she strove to find again if married. Etta played on the floor with the four half-siblings, whom she adored. The oldest, Maryann, was six years younger, followed by Harry, Jr., Mark, and Robert, twelve years younger. Another would be born a year before Etta left for Chicago, one she never really got to know–Nancy–whom everyone called Mona, young enough to be her daughter.

* * *

Ah, married—how could that ever happen now? The attraction to Mr. Andrews had intensified, and she sensed perhaps he felt the same way but knew that with his position in society, a marriage between them, could never happen. Unless . . .

Settling In

Life at the bordello seemed to be becoming normal to Etta. The days, weeks, then months flew by as she formed deeper friendships with the other girls, learned one fork from another, when to use 'who' or 'whom,' how to walk gracefully, sit demurely, and even how to properly don and remove a fur coat. Everything new excited her. She loved learning the finer points of the upper class's etiquette and lifestyle. She pored over her copy of the newly published *Complete Etiquette for Ladies*, searching for little-known rules of behavior. The theater and concerts opened new worlds of make-believe, sound, and fantasy.

One day at breakfast, Katie spoke up. "I had an invitation last night from one of my clients."

"Who? What?" her companions chortled in unison.

"Well, I can't tell you who, but he told me he has a friend who owned Henrici's Restaurant–and he said he could get us in for supper one evening."

All had heard of the exclusive dining favorite of Chicago society. Excitement rippled around the table.

"When?"

"Well, if y'all are free this Saturday. We could be home by nine if we go early."

"What are you going to wear?" Katie asked Etta as they rose from the table.

"Hmmm... I'll have to give that some thought," replied Etta. My first time out in public with the girls, she thought.

Promptly at five-thirty that Saturday, the girls mounted a carriage, bubbling with excitement. In just a few blocks, the group arrived at the exclusive restaurant.

"I'm starved!" yelled Katie as she dismounted and took her place at the head of the line. The group entered the foyer.

In a moment, the matre'd appeared. "Yes?" he inquired.

"We're here at the invitation of Mr. Blanchard," stated Katie primly. "I believe he made a reservation for us—for we—I mean, us, five."

The matre'd looked the girls up and down. Most had worn their gaudiest gowns, and all but Etta had painted their faces with charcoal and poppy petals.

He walked to the podium and opened a dark green leather-bound book. "I don't see your name here, ma'am. What was it again?"

Katie replied, teeth set, speaking each syllable clearly. "Kath-e-rine Ba-ker."

He looked again, then stepped out, blocking their way into the restaurant. "Apologies, ma'am, I see no reservation under that name."

Katie began to object.

"I'm sorry, ladies, but we have other customers waiting. You are going to have to leave."

While they were arguing, Etta had leaned over the podium and saw the name clearly: 'Katherine Baker'.

Fury surrounded them as the women made their way

back onto the street. Their voices blended into an arcane chorus of objections, like chattering chickadees.

"Who does he think he is!"

"Well, I never!"

"Wait til I see that client again; I'm going to give him a piece of my mind!"

Doubt filled Etta's mind as she wondered about this rejection. She suspected her friends' flashy clothes and make-up were the root cause of the debacle but couldn't be sure. That old feeling of being tossed aside again engulfed her. Do businesses have the right to do that, she wondered.

The girls made it back to the bordello in time for supper.

New Challenges

Etta's new occupation had its challenges. She had always made her own gowns unless she could buy them used, but they were simple compared to the elegant frocks now coming to life in her hands. Amazed at the yardage needed for each garment, she felt grateful Madame's store of fabrics more than adequately met the fashion needs of the active women in the bordello.

Attaching all the extra pieces to the dresses served as her most challenging task—flounces, collars, hems, and fancy sleeves-- buttons, laces, bustles, and pleats. All cried out for extra time and attention to their careful construction.

Ideas for designs were not lacking. Patterns for elaborate gowns filled one large drawer, and the girls often came to Etta with a description or drawing of a dress they had seen and wanted to be copied. When she fell asleep on her little cot, dreams of fabric-wielding scissors in fights with long rulers filled her nights.

And there were mistakes. She finished Grace's ball gown first–red velvet– with lace and flounces abounding. As per the custom, she basted the hem on for easy removal for cleaning.

The day after the ball, Etta meticulously sewed beading on a blue satin gown when Lizzie entered the room.

"Etta, are you in trouble," she warned.

How could I get into trouble working in such a benign profession?

"Grace's hem came loose at the ball; she tripped on it while dancing and broke her leg. Now she is in a cast, can't work, and is blaming you for shoddy work."

Etta slumped. My first job and I failed.

"She's telling all the other girls about what an amateur you are and accusing you for her losing her nightly wages."

Her relationship with Grace suffered from then on, and the other girls' friendships seemed cooler, but Etta loved her work and improved daily. What a change from the dull task of creating a man's suit, she thought. She immersed herself in the beauty of the rich fabrics, soft velvets, crisp laces, and delicate tulles. Creativity seemed like mother's milk to her, and soon the exclamations of the girls when she delivered her masterpieces to them brought her the rewards. She avoided Grace.

The Gypsy

Etta decided to visit Madam Vertina since she had heard about the seer's talents from the girls a few months after her arrival at Martha Webster's. On her first visit, she looked around nervously, having heard frightening tales of witchcraft about fortune-telling, but wanted to know her future. A coin she had collected from David was safely secured in her purse.

Candles glowed within the room of the gypsy's apartment, giving it a mysterious ambiance. After a few moments, curtains at a dark end of the room parted, and a wrinkled old woman entered, dressed in a purple shift, gathered at the waist by a rope of beads, a multi-colored striped scarf covering her gray head and extending past her waist. Beads hung from its edges, and an odd-looking symbol of gold hung at her throat. A large woman, slightly bent, she shuffled over to a small table. She did not smile—she barely glanced at Etta before taking her seat opposite. "You, sit." She pointed to the chair across from her. Her voice sounded as deep as a canyon.

Etta sat down, and the gypsy extended her hand.

Etta stared. What was she supposed to do? Hold her hand? Read her palm? Oh! She suddenly realized. She wants to be paid. Etta reached into her purse, extracted the coin, and laid it in the woman's hand.

The gypsy slowly looked up. A few wild hairs were trying to escape her colorful scarf. She took in Etta's dress, tiny hands, and face, staring at her for what felt like forever to Etta, who began to squirm. The woman put out her hand again, not looking up at Etta.

"Give me hand, my dear," she said.

Which hand? Etta wondered but quickly placed her right hand on the worn table, partially covered with a paisley scarf.

The woman continued to stare at Etta. After what seemed like forever, she looked down without blinking and took Etta's hand.

She examined the palm as though she were planning a worldwide trip, line by line, crease by crease. Etta suddenly felt self-conscious. Were her nails trimmed and clean? She hadn't thought to check them when she left for the visit.

Finally, the woman looked up and spoke. "Ah, my dear," she paused. "You had sad life." She shook her head. "Very sad. Poor little thing, no joys many take for granted." Her finger slowly traced along the lines of Etta's hand. The woman spoke with a strong foreign accent, but Etta understood most of the words.

"Hmmm." She let go of Etta's hand. She sat back, put her hands on her lap, and looked up at her client.

She went on. "Much deception. Many people lie to you, lead you down wrong paths. Great suffering. You wonder why put in this life when others are blessed and happy." The seer shook her head. So far, the gypsy hadn't told Etta anything she didn't already know.

"You strong. You know what want. What you no realize you now in charge of life. You grown woman, make own choices now. Have great power. Must learn use it." With that, she abruptly rose and disappeared through the curtains.

Etta sat still. Is she coming back? Can't I ask any questions? Is this all nonsense, and have I wasted my time and money? Have I been a fool? The clock in the room ticked louder. Etta left.

She turned her face against the blast out on the streets, absentmindedly bumping into people as her thoughts chased each other 'round and 'round in her mind like the Chicago wind buffeting the corners of the city. Unaware of the chill or the street sounds around her, she thought, what did the reading mean, and how will I get this power? What do I have to do? But most of all, whom could she trust to teach her?

Adrift

Winter melted into spring, and the brighter tulle and organza fabrics eclipsed the heavy velvets and satins at the sewing table. But still, contentment evaded Etta. A tiny voice in her mind kept asking, is this all?

Etta had few opportunities to meet men. She rarely went upstairs after supper as she wanted no part of the nightly goings-on. She still had a lingering fear that someday, she would end up working in the upstairs profession. And loneliness surrounded her with a darker pall than she had ever known. She felt adrift in the sea of the life around her. She tried not to think of how isolated and rudderless she felt and how marriage continued to elude her.

She often turned to David Andrews. He now visited regularly, having convinced Madame that he could have his suits made by Etta. The shrewd Madame knew he could open more doors to Chicago society for her. How did he manage that? And why? What did he offer her, Etta wondered.

The Gloves

David dropped by to pick up his new suit and showed his pleasure by turning, commenting, and smiling in the mirror at his final fitting.

"Miss Etta," he asked. "I'm already thinking of my summer wardrobe. Would you be kind enough to accompany me to the haberdashery to help me pick a fabric for my next suit?"

A thrill ran through Etta's body. She rarely had a chance to get out of the house. She enthusiastically agreed, and the couple hailed a carriage to Gent's at 98 Wabash Street. As tshe stepped inside the store, the smell of the masculine materials immediately rushed her back to Pittsburgh, the tailor shop, the long hours, and the accompanying horrid pay.

The pair walked around the shop, voices low, handling and commenting on the fabrics. They settled on a lightweight seersucker in pale blue.

"This will go nicely with your coloring," Etta told David. She blushed, concerned that he may have discerned how closely she had been observing him.

He smiled, nodded, and directed the clerk to measure the fabric.

After the purchase, David invited her to join him for a glass of mulled cider in a small shop nearby.

This feels like something other than a business meeting, she thought.

The couple sat at a small round table in the corner. "Tell me about yourself, Etta." David offered.

"What would you like to know, Mr. Andrews?"

"David, please, David."

"All right, Mr. Andrews, David it is." They both laughed. The couple seemed so right together; both loved humor and were quite funny, each in their own right.

"Tell me about your family."

"Well, my papa married a girl from Scotland. I'm not sure where they met, but they now have five children. Three boys and two girls–and live in Pennsylvania."

Amazing, thought David. The same as me. "How about your mother?"

"Etta paused. There it was, that ugly question again. "I never knew my mother. I know she came to this country from Ireland and was Catholic, and my father was Protestant, so their parents wouldn't allow them to marry. They must have been very much in love," she added.

"So you never knew your mother?"

"No." Etta fell silent.

How amazingly similar our childhoods were, David thought. He could relate to her pain, as his mother had died just days after his birth. He and Etta were the only children of their parents. Each had lost their mother at birth. He also had a stepmother and five half-siblings.

Etta continued, "When Nana Agnes died, I was thirteen. My aunt and uncle, who also lived with us, wanted me to leave, so my papa sent me to a family in Pittsburgh. That couple was quite young, and after their first child, they asked me to leave school and learn a trade. Then I was on my own."

She cleared her throat. His questions were leading into dangerous territory. She despised anyone prying into her past.

"And what brought you to Chicago?"

Etta replied without hesitation what she had memorized. "I met a marvelous man in Pittsburgh, we married and moved here, but shortly afterward, he was killed in an accident."

David looked down at his glass. What a sad tale. He ached for this young girl. He wanted to get up, approach her, and put his arms around her, but propriety ruled. Every cell in David's body begged to reach out to her, touch her, and make her his own. But the deafening rules of convention were halting his action.

Losing Nana

Talking to David about her childhood made Etta reminisce about her days on the farm in Pennsylvania. Just thirteen, she lived with her beloved Nana, her aunt Mary and uncle Paul Adair.

* * *

One hot morning in 1870, Aunt Mary nudged her. "Henrietta, get up." Her aunt only called her 'Henrietta' when something was amiss.

"What?" Etta groggily tried to remember what her latest crime was.

As a young girl, she'd been cursed with a bad temper. The Adair household had become accustomed to her tantrums. She would slam doors, throw things, scream, and yell if something didn't go her way.

"Something's happened. Come down right away." She slipped on her shift, slid into her shoes, and ran downstairs. Everyone sat still in the parlor. No one spoke. After a glance at Etta, they turned away and looked down at the floor. Etta noticed Nana's closed door. The doctor stood nearby, stuffing his stethoscope into his worn leather bag.

"Where's Nana? What happened? Where's Nana?"

A long silence. No one moved.

"Nana's gone with the Lord." murmured her uncle.

"She's at peace now." added Aunt Mary.

Etta sat down hard on the bottom step. The hands on the grandfather clock seemed to slow and tick louder. Was she dreaming? Maybe if she went back to bed, she would be back in that hazy field with Papa, and all this would disappear. Why were the grownups not wailing and screaming? She dug her nail into the rough stair and pulled out a splinter of wood. An ant crawled toward her shoe. She blocked its path with her foot, watched it turn away, ground it under her shoe, turned, and ran upstairs.

The doctor nodded goodbye to everyone.

"Thank you, Doc, for coming out so early," said Uncle Paul. "We'll make all the necessary arrangements. Here's a dozen eggs for the Missus."

Attempted Murder

The snow silently dusted the filth of the Chicago streets with white. Etta heard it swallowing the street sounds outside her lower-level window. The few footfalls outside made crunch-crunch sounds, some slower, some faster; the horses' hooves stumbled in the snow and sounded muffled. Busy at work, she attempted to cut a piece of satin on the bias to make a pleated ruffle hem.

The slippery fabric kept sliding off the table onto the floor, so she had to start over again. Finally, with a yell of rage, she threw the scissors against the wall. They landed in the bosom of the dress form just as she heard an "ahem" behind her. She had not heard David's steps on the stairs.

"Well, you at least have good aim," he said with a chuckle.

Embarrassment flooded through Etta. While she had been ill, her weakness prevented her from having her usual temper tantrums, but it had been several weeks since her full recovery, and her strength of body and character had returned.

"Don't worry, Miss, your secret is mine," he added warmly.

Etta blushed. "Good morning, Mr. Andrews."

"David, please, Miss."

He walked over to the fallen mannequin and bent down. "Do you think she is dead?" he said with a twinkle in his eye. "Or do you think we can revive her?"

The pair bent down to right the dress form when their hands touched. David caught her gaze and held it as something electric passed between them. Then, just as suddenly, they both stood up and wielded the form back to its place.

An awkward silence followed. Each knew what had just happened; it excited David, and Etta flustered. What is the next step?

The Visit

"Etta, you have a note," Molly called down the stairs. Etta ran up and tore it open.

"Katie," she shouted up the stairs to the second floor. With Madame out, she would not be scolded for yelling in the house. "Guess what–David is going to take me to see his parent's house–in the Lake View district. I've always wanted to see it."

"I thought you told me you didn't think he would ever take you there," replied Katie with a frown.

"All his family is away," Etta said. "He's calling for me this afternoon at two." Etta ran downstairs to dress for the special occasion, giddy with excitement.

And that is how it came to be, promptly at two o'clock on a clear Sunday afternoon in May of 1877, Henrietta Ware, a lonely soul from Pittsburgh, entered the stately home of James J. Andrews, Sr. The house took its place along a long line of Chicago mansions–a neighborhood so exclusive that none had street names or house numbers; people called it simply, 'Lake View'.

Etta stared at the house—one of the most beautiful she

had ever seen—with tall Corinthian columns and wide double front doors topped by an ornate cornice. Colorful tulips led up to the wide stairs. David helped her down from the hansom, up the stairs, and pulled open the heavy walnut doors.

Etta's eyes were first drawn to the entry hall oil paintings of sublime woods, hazy green fields, and contented cows hanging on the maroon taffeta walls.

"This is our latest acquisition," David lovingly stroked the ornate gold frame of a Corot.

Etta spotted the sterling silver tray for calling cards and a leather-bound guest book. "Shall I sign it?" Etta giggled.

"No!" David said with a laugh. "Don't you dare!" He grabbed her and held her close. "Now you behave, y'hear?"

Etta loved it when David used the gentlemanly Southern way of talking. After being away from Virginia for several years, he still had a slight drawl.

"Come down here." He took her hand and led her downstairs io the armory room. "This is our collection of Kentucky long rifles. Aren't they beauties?" His face beamed as he gazed upon the impressive collection. Hung in between the rifles on the walls were paintings of hunting scenes—red coats flashing against green fields, spotted beagles, and dappled horses.

A long table dominated the center of the room, covered with green oilcloth and tools for cleaning the rifles. Tall stools banked the sides of the table. Oily and metallic odors dominated the room.

"Can you shoot them?" Etta asked, nodding at the rifles. "Can I shoot them!" David boomed. "Honey, how do you think we ate? Somebody had to bring home the bacon. And the game was just outside, waiting to be brought down and in for supper."

"You mean DEER, Dear." Etta laughed.

"Yes, indeed," David replied, remembering his wonderful shooting excursions. "Yup. Those were the days. And I loved hunting with my father and brothers."

Etta grew quiet. David had finally mentioned his family. Most of what she had heard about the Chicago Andrews family she had gleaned from the newspapers and local gossip.

David slid the upstairs pocket doors wide and led her into the dining room. Etta had never seen such art. Hunting scenes—acres of green fields with fat livestock and glimmering country streams looked down on an enormous, ornate walnut table flanked by twenty chairs over a blue Aubusson rug. Giant palms enlivened every corner. Silk draperies with ornate bouillon tassels flanked the floor-to-ceiling windows. A life-sized marble sculpture of a naked Adonis stood in the corner, silently observing the Andrews' elegant dinner parties occurring nearly every weekend. She walked over to the statue and ran her hand along his flanks.

David held up his hand. "Don't touch, Love."

Etta flushed. Suddenly she felt like a four-year-old caught wetting the bed. No matter how much training Martha Webster had provided, reprimands like this would bring her back to her humble roots. Don't touch the bronze, don't say 'they done,' and don't slurp the soup. Don't, Don't, Don't. A cultural wall existed that she would never be able to scale. She pinched her arm to return to the present time.

She then remembered an incident just a few weeks after she arrived at the bordello when, at supper, Louisa told a story about a rambunctious client the night before. Etta, entranced by the story, didn't notice she had licked the butter knife of its jam until silver forks clattering on porcelain plates jarred her focus. Everyone stared. She looked around the table, the butter knife still in her mouth, and, when she realized what she had done, blushed and placed the knife back down on her bread plate. Then everyone laughed, and the world once again righted itself.

David ushered her into the library. She looked around at an enormous leather-topped carved desk and chair, sterling silver inkwell, blotter, and neatly stacked papers. Etta had never seen so many books shelved on every wall, floor to ceiling. She ran her fingers along the red, dark green, and maroon books and read the authors—Shakespeare, Goethe, Milton. Who were these people?

"David, have you read all of these?"

David chuckled, "Of course not, but we've all read many of them," David said, looking fondly at Etta, reveling in her wonderment.

"Oh, my," was all she could say, suddenly feeling ignorant.

"What's this one?" She pulled a slim volume off the shelf. She turned the book sideways and read the title of *The Scarlet Letter* aloud.

David pulled her close to him. "One of my favorites, Love. Someday I will read it to you."

"I do know how to read, you know, David. I finished eighth grade."

David put his mouth near her ear and whispered, "I know, Dearest, but this book is special so I want to share it with you." He placed the book back on the shelf.

"Let me show you upstairs," David grabbed her hand again and led her toward the curved staircase to the second floor, to his bedroom.

Apprehension flooded Etta. She suspected what going upstairs with him entailed. But *isn't this what I wanted?*

Isn't this how I take charge of my destiny? She was torn, and hesitated.

David held out his hand, and Etta acquiesced. On the second stair, she paused under a large oil portrait.

"Is this one of your people?" she inquired, trying to stall.

"Yes, Love, that is my grand-pappy. He came to Virginia after the Scots lost the battle at Culloden. He and his brother both fought there. That was in 1746."

"Culloden?" She inquired. "I think I've heard of it. Is it a big city?"

Exasperation hit David. He often forgot what a sheltered life his love had led. "No, Dear, it's a battlefield in Scotland, where my family originated. My great-grand-pappy and his brother fled to America after losing the battle."

The couple continued up the stairs. David opened a door on the right.

"Is this your room?" Etta queried. Her nerves prevented her from fully taking in the room.

"Yes, ma'am, it 'shore is."

She looked around and tried to imagine his living there, dressing, sleeping, bathing, the intimacies of his life to which she could never be a party. She walked over to the window to delay the inevitable. Suddenly she felt him behind her as he took her in his embrace.

He drew her close, taking in her marvelous fragrance, and began unlacing her dress. "Etta, I've wanted this since the first day I laid eyes on you. You are the woman of my life, and I knew it then. I want you here, in my bed, with me, my love, so I can think of you every evening as I fall asleep."

A flutter ran through her as her body awakened to her

lover's touch. He led her to the giant four-poster bed and drew back the silk comforter. Etta began to tremble as he gently lowered her onto the smooth silken sheets.

David's shock at taking Etta's virginity stunned him. After all, she had been introduced to him as the widow of Charles King, and she worked in a bordello. What is going on?

"Did I hurt you?" he asked.

"No, not really, Darling. Don't give it another thought."

He did give it a second thought. And another. Bewildered by this mystery of a girl he had just bedded, he had much to learn about her mysterious past. But not now.

They had just finished their love-making and had dozed off when they heard the click of a key in a lock and the front door opening.

"HUSH," David whispered. "Here, hide in here," he instructed as he opened the mirrored door of his ornately carved cedar-lined wardrobe.

Etta struggled in as David grabbed a dressing gown and threw it on. Etta, silent as she was naked, hid, wedged between his opera shoes and hunting boots, inhaling the scent of cedar. Her heart beating wildly, she remained quiet among the beautiful smoking jackets and formal wear hanging about her.

"Peter?" She heard David say. "What's my little brother doing here?"

"I'm home for the summer from Yale. What are you doing here, David?" his sibling shot back.

"I have an appointment later and just stopped to pick up some things. I decided to take a little rest while I was here." A lie, as David rarely visited the house. "Anyway, welcome home, we'll have to have lunch to catch up."

As Etta would later learn, David had never been wholly

accepted into the Andrews family, even though he was the eldest son. After all, as a half-brother, he never quite fit in with the stellar pedigrees of his younger siblings, whose mother was a descendant of a Virginia governor and Confederate general.

As was the custom of the day, the Andrews children lived with their parents until they married. But David maintained the suite at the Palmer House.

After David heard the front door slam shut, he called out, with a nervous laugh, "You can come out now, Dearest. My word, that was a close call!"

Etta's legs were cramped, and she felt chilled after sitting naked in the wardrobe. After dressing, the couple descended the stairs to the bright, airy kitchen in the rear of the house.

"How about some tea? I'll have to make it since the servants have been given the weekend off. I'll try not to poison you," he said with a chuckle. After pouring a shot of bourbon into his cup, he heated some cranberry scones the cook had left in the larder and put out unsalted butter.

Etta remembered to butter the scone, one bite at a time. She thought I'll bet no one had to teach David how to butter his bread. I could sit here forever; I'm in heaven. She had an idea while looking out at the scarlet geraniums adorning the window sills and the carefully tended gardens. I can create a new life! A life that will take me out of the Levee District into this rarefied world of oriental rugs, servants, and Corot paintings of pristine English countrysides.

Suddenly they heard a key in the kitchen door lock. David jumped, his look one of alarm. They both froze.

The door opened.

Meeting Sallie Reed

"Sallie! How nice to see you," David said with a terse smile. "What are you doing here on a Sunday?" His voice sounded less than confident.

"Well, good afternoon, Mista David! What a surprise!" The immense cook for the Andrews family waddled into the airy kitchen. "I'm here to get ready for tomorrow. Mizz Nancy's having ten for lunch, and I gotta get these butterfly rolls going. How you been? Ain't seen you around in a while."

"Very well, Sallie, it's good to see you, too." David repeated. He cleared his throat, looked down at the floor, and shuffled his feet. "Henrietta, I'd like you to meet our family cook, Sallie Reed."

"Well, it's a pleasure, Miss Henrietta, welcome to the Andrews house." Sallie's smile seemed to embrace the couple.

Still uncertain of how to speak to servants, Etta smiled and nodded. She stood and whispered to David, who murmured something and gestured. She stepped out.

After she had relieved herself, she returned to the kitchen to find David gone.

"Where's David?" she queried.

"Oh, somebody at the front door, Miss Etta," Sallie replied. She shuffled to the pantry, large bowl in hand. Etta followed Sallie and leaned against the door. Even though Martha Webster fed a dozen people daily, the Andrews pantry looked nearly as large as the one at Martha's. Etta marveled at the stores it held. She leaned back and peeked into the adjoining butler's pantry, noting the shelves filled with Limoges china and crystal glasses with wide gold scalloped borders. Etta watched Sallie scoop the flour from the flour bin into the bowl.

"Have you worked for the Andrews's long?"

"Oh, Lordy, Miss Etta, I sure have. I was called back in Virginia when poor David lost his mama when he were born. His big brother Willie—he were four—couldn't figure out what was happening, with his new baby brother bawling all the time and their mama moaning and groaning on the bed. I took baby David, nursed him, tended to them two, and loved 'em like my own," She chuckled. "And look at Mista David now, a fine, grown man."

"I didn't realize David had an older brother."

"Well, that poor boy Willie died—he were only eleven. The fever, y' know. Such a shame. He were a quiet boy—the oldest of the Andrews sons. You known Mista David long?"

Etta didn't answer at first. She cleared her throat and picked at a hangnail.

"We met last fall," said Etta softly. Please, no more questions!

Etta felt a warm connection to this warm woman. She watched as Sallie measured the flour into the bowl, added

Fleischman's yeast and water, and kneaded the ball into submission. The flour dusted over Sallie's massive arms.

Etta put her head down and turned her face away. The sight and smell of the dough reminded her of the kitchen at the farm and how she would sit by her beloved nana while she made bread. She brushed at her eyes.

"Well, sort of, I guess. I'm new to Chicago, been here just a few months, and David and I met soon after I got arrived." She stopped, fearing Sallie would ask her how they met. She cleared her throat. "Well, I guess I'd better find him. I have to get back." She arose and headed towards the front door. Thank you for telling me about David's childhood. It means a lot to me. I care quite a bit for him."

"Well, that's nice, Miss Etta. I do, too. Y'all come back, y'hear?" and flashed her a smile, then turned back to her kneading, her heavy shoulders heaving up and down as her knuckles forced grooves in the thick ball of dough.

Etta approached the front door, where David waved goodbye to a man mounting his horse. "Who was that, David?" she asked.

"Oh, just a neighbor." He rarely shared details of his life with her. Once again, she felt abandoned and shut out. But soon, that is all going to change. She had made up her mind.

David helped her into the carriage. "I'm staying here a while, Etta. I have some work to do."

Another rejection. I had hoped we could spend the entire day together. She began planning on the ride back from Lake View to Clark Street. She thought—

I am going to change everything. A slow smile crept over her face—I will have a new life—no more feeling like an outsider.

The Plan

Long afternoon shadows greeted Etta's arrival at the bordello that Sunday afternoon.

She alighted, holding her skirt up over the muddy street with one hand, as the etiquette book had taught her. Imbued with a new air of confidence, she ran up the steps to the front door.

Rushing out was her friend, Katie. "Hey, Etta, how was it? You've been gone a long time," she snickered suggestively.

"It was marvelous," she replied, blushing unexpectantly, and grinned. "Wait 'til I tell you what I've decided to do." She started to go on, but Katie stopped her.

"Sorry, but gotta run, meeting someone. Stop by my room later, all right?" And away she went, dashing after a carriage.

Etta felt like a deflated balloon. She so wanted to share her plan. She passed Madame, who gave her a nod on her way in. And goodbye to you, Etta thought. Goodbye to all your filthy business and this life.

After retiring to her sewing room, she lay on her cot,

allowing her mind to drift back to that magic hour when David made her his. Shock and disappointment had accompanied his entry. Sex is supposed to feel good! But it hurt and wasn't at all pleasant. She had held her breath, hoping the pleasure would follow, but it never arrived. All these years of 'saving myself', and this is the result? Why did women continue participating in this act, she wondered. But now that isn't important. What is important is that I am following the gypsy's advice and taking control of my life by creating a new one.

The Park

A couple of weeks later, in June 1877, David and Etta relaxed on a bench in Lincoln Park, enjoying the long summer evening. A soothing fresh northerly breeze from the lake had sent the nasty stockyard odors packing. Etta sipped a glass of fresh lemonade bought from a youthful vendor while David enjoyed a cigar.

Etta spoke. "It was nice meeting your family cook, Sallie, the other day."

"Yes, that was a surprise," David replied. He fell silent, recalling being raised by the warm, loving woman.

"Is she a good cook?" Asked Etta. Sometimes getting conversation out of her lover seemed like pulling teeth.

"Oh, yes," David laughed. "You should taste her biscuits."

He fell silent again. Sometimes Etta wanted to grab his head and shake it, shouting, "Hello! Is there anyone in there?" But she didn't dare. Her relationship with him felt as fragile as a spider web in a storm. She would not brush against it causing her hopes to collapse into a tangled mess.

She had too many dreams for her future with him. Soon, her plan would bring them all to fruition.

* * *

David silently revisited his childhood in Virginia as he recalled the shards of shock and pain at the loss of his older brother. Will, just eleven, had been a pillar of strength for the motherless David, who was five at the time. Their mother, Jane Parker, had been a lovely, child-like southern beauty when she married James Andrews. James adored the sweet and tender southern belle and fell into prolonged silences and rages after her death from childbed fever at David's birth. She was twenty-three.

* * *

"Father set Sallie free, you know—even before the War." David's sudden statement jolted Etta back to reality. The warm afternoon air had caressed her brow and had made her nod off. A lonely cloud drifted across the sun, swallowing the sharp summer shadows.

"That's nice," murmured Etta. She hoped he would continue and shook herself awake.

* * *

David's silent musings continued. As he grew older, he increasingly felt that his father blamed him for the death of his beloved wife. Three years later, when his father remarried, that belief filtered down to his stepmother like bluebells spreading over Virginia lands. Stepmother Nancy never demonstrated unkindness towards little David. She was polite but cool, growing more so whenever she brought more half-siblings into David's world.

* * *

David tapped his cigar ashes onto the grass. He turned away, gazing over the shimmering lake, recalling pressing his little head between Sallie Reed's warm breasts. He could still remember the rhythm of the creaking rocker next to the wood stove and the smell of warm bread filling his young nostrils and wafting over his tears.

* * *

David stood. "Must leave, Darling. I'll walk you home."

The Attack

A few days later, Etta needed to drop off Louisa's dress before the bordello opened-only minutes away. She decided to use the front stairs to save time, a forbidden route for her as a servant. As she neared the front door, a loud rap startled her. Etta looked around, expecting to see Arthur round the corner at any minute to usher in the first guest of the evening. He was nowhere in sight.

The door shot open as she approached the first stair landing, and a large, rough-looking man burst in the door. He grinned at her, grabbed her arm, yelling with glee as he dragged her up the stairs. "Yes, siree, my dearie. You are perfect. I've heard about this place-I'm from Milwaukee, and you are just what I've been looking for."

The shock of the attack rendered Etta speechless. He pulled her into the first empty room, threw her on the bed, and unbuttoned his pants. Throwing his body on top of her, he began ripping off her clothes. Her screams sprang to life and spread throughout the house like wildfire in a dry forest.

Heavy footsteps pounded up the stairs, and the door burst open just as the rape was about to take place. Arthur grabbed the intruder and threw him out into the hall, tossing his clothes after him. "Get out of here," he boomed. "And never come back. We don't cater to such things in this house."

Etta sat up on the bed, her clothes in tatters. Sobbing, she tried to cover herself as Madame appeared at the door.

"How did he get in, Arthur?" she shouted. "Don't you know incidents like this can ruin our reputation? I cannot tell you how furious I am."

Arthur said, "I don't know. I didn't let him in, Ma'am."

"And Etta, where did he find you?"

Etta held her face in her hands as she sobbed. She couldn't think of a reply. Madame sent Arthur downstairs to ensure the assailant had left.

She sat down by Etta. "Henrietta, I am so sorry. This kind of thing is never supposed to happen in my establishment. Someone must have left the door unlocked."

The savvy owner knew it had to be Katie, as she had been assigned to put out the rose placard at nine, then lock the door every morning at four. Later, Etta heard Madame docked Katie's wages for a week.

"I will find this man!" Madame whispered to herself. "And he'll never terrorize another woman." Livid, she sent a note to the police chief. She had Etta and Arthur give the police a good description of the attacker. The police discovered the man had a prior record of assault, among other crimes. They knew him well and his whereabouts.

Several weeks later, someone found his body floating in the Chicago River and notified the authorities. No investigation ever followed.

The Evidence

Now that David had possessed his love, his passion snowballed. When he visited Etta for a fitting or repair, it seemed natural to lead her over to the little cot in the corner. David wanted her entirely, wholly. He couldn't get enough of her. He often found his mind drifting back to her lovely body in the middle of a business transaction, in the dentist's chair, and even in church while singing *Onward, Christian Soldiers*.

The next time the couple found themselves together, David noticed her bruises. He held up her arm. "What happened?" he said with concern.

She looked down at the marks from the attack. "Oh, I'd nearly forgotten about that." She forced a laugh. She tried to think of an excuse but—put on the spot—couldn't think of a thing to explain the bruises. "Oh, it's nothing," she said, "just a little fall. I tripped over something." She pulled David toward her. "Don't worry about it. Here, kiss me."

Her explanation did not satisfy David, and he began wondering what else went on at the bordello he didn't know about.

"And you seem so nervous lately. Has something happened?"

Etta turned her head and choked back a sob. "I've not been sleeping well. My nights are filled with horrid dreams," she replied.

"Oh, come here, Dearest. I'm so sorry," he said as he held her closer. "My poor, poor girl." He hated to see his love so unhappy. Her eyes were closed, and he hugged her closer. "I wish I could make it go away," he whispered as he soothed her and stroked her hair.

David never brought up the subject again.

The Kitten

Sadie had rescued a kitten, although she knew Madame, who viewed all pets as dirty, would disapprove. Sadie hid it in her room. The outdoor air smelled so noxious that no one could smell anything worse inside the bordello, not even a cat box. Cracking open a window quickly overpowered any indoor odors. The city's putrid air would seek out every nook and cranny and cling to the room fabrics like flies on honey.

All white, with four black hairs atop her head, the kitten looked like a ball of fuzz. When Etta saw it, she immediately fell in love with its bright blue eyes, pink nose and ears, and tiny tongue. She gathered it up and snuggled it to her neck. "Oh, I LOVE HER!" she exclaimed. Etta often stopped by Sadie's room and played with the soft furry treasure whenever Sadie was out. She even took it downstairs to her bed to play with and revel in its warmth and softness.

Was this what it felt like to hold a baby? She had held her half-brothers and sisters as infants, but this seemed different. This creature brought constant joy and pleasure to Etta.

One morning, as she delivered a dress to Lizzie, she heard a terrible mewing. She stopped, cocked her head, and listened again. No doubt. She heard the kitten. She looked at Sadie's closed door, behind from which came the mewing, sounding distressed and weak.

Opening the door, Etta beheld the ratty-looking creature as it crept weakly toward her. The food bowl sat empty, and the water bowl looked bone dry.

Etta gathered up the kitten and crept down the back stairs to the kitchen to find scraps. On returning to her workplace, she held the kitten, feeding it with her fingers, nuzzling and petting it as she watched it swallow each morsel. Etta kept the kitten all night in the drawer holding soft pom-poms.

The next day the little creature had brightened a bit. At breakfast, Etta casually asked, "Anyone seen Sadie?"

Lizzie looked up and stared at her. "You haven't heard?" she asked. Etta shook her head. Living in the basement, caused her to miss out on much of the gossip.

"No. What's happened? Is she away?" Etta tried to appear uninterested, not looking up as she spooned oatmeal with fresh strawberries into her mouth. Lizzie looked around the table, then down.

Louisa piped up. "You knew, Etta, Sadie got herself pregnant."

"No." Etta was genuinely surprised. "She said nothing to me!"

"Yes, well, she decided not to have it, so she paid a visit to Dr. N. C."

Everyone knew of Doctor N. C. He helped the bordellos by providing end-of-pregnancy services to unfortunate girls. Called simply 'Dr. N. C.,' no one ever said his full name.

The wind howled outside, and the shutters rattled. Etta looked up, waiting for an answer.

"Lizzie spoke quietly. "It didn't go well. We're taking up a collection. Her funeral is tomorrow."

Doctor N. C.

Always so careful with her sponges and douches, Sadie had found herself devastated when she became pregnant. Although she always wanted a family, now was not the time.

She met Madame in her office and gave her the bad news.

"Thank you for coming to me," Madame told her. "I'll make all the arrangements. After all, I do want you to stay on."

One week later, Sadie stepped down from the carriage at Dr. N.C.'s office. After waiting nearly an hour, the doctor greeted her.

"Welcome, Miss Sadie," he said with a smile. "Come in," and led her to a small room in the back. "Please remove your undergarments and lie down on the table."

Sadie did as told. When she looked up, a shock bolted through her. The doctor had his trousers down and was poised for sex.

"What are you doing?" she yelled.

"Do you want this procedure or not?" said the doctor

gruffly. "Now be quiet and spread your legs. Or you can find someone else to take care of your problem."

After the attack, the doctor redressed and proceeded with the abortion.

The amount of pain the extraction caused surprised Sadie. Dr. N. C. performed it without giving her an opiate. Afterward, she sat in a chair for nearly an hour before being released.

Head in hands, she shuddered from the dual attacks on her body. Blood and tears merged in a river of anguish. Why is it men think it acceptable to rape brothel workers?

Sadie felt every cobblestone on the carriage ride home. It seemed as though her insides would spill out onto the leather seat. She tried fighting her tears, but they gushed once she reached the bordello. Madame tended to her pain and distress by giving her small doses of laudanum, a potion the girls kept by their bedsides.

At least now the poor girl will sleep, Madame thought. But the infection had already begun its fatal ravaging of Sadie's body.

The New Girls

Etta stood in the library at the bordello, looking for a copy of *The Scarlet Letter*. Not knowing the author, her fingers inched along the shelves and danced on the spines of the books.

"Etta!" Katie's shout shattered the stillness of the room. "I've been looking for you! Have you seen the new girls?"

Madame's plans for her facility were ambitious. She hoped to employ at least twenty-five girls by the end of 1877. The expansion of the building had begun in earnest. By fall, several new faces graced the halls of the Clark Street establishment.

"They're twins," can you imagine? What do you suppose Madame's plans for them are?" Katie laughed uproariously.

Passers-by on the streets often stopped to stare at Millie and Billie, identical twins. Flaxen-haired and petite at just sixteen, they had pert noses and robin's-egg blue eyes. The twins rooming together provided the perfect setup for Madame's clients interested in a threesome, and the pair were in great demand by the more adventuresome clients.

"Their stepfather is that client with the funny mustache-you must have seen him-you know-he visits Louisa. I heard he negotiated what he thought would be a swap with Madame for a lower fee. He traded his twins for services! Can you imagine?" The girls dashed out to get a look at the new doves.

Madame suppressed a smile as she noticed Gisela's references in hand in the bordello office. The gloomy day hinted at winter. "I won't need that," Madame told her laughingly. Thrilled there was no commission to pay one of her recruiters, she hired her on the spot.

Gisela had an illegitimate son being raised by her mother. Stocky and tall, Gesila was the oldest of the new girls at twenty-six. Her loud guffaws made her easy to find in the facility. At breakfast her first day, she enlivened the meal with her bawdy sense of humor, stories told with a thick German accent.

"I really like her!" whispered Grace. "She's going to add a lot of fun to our group." Everyone nodded in agreement between sips of hot, steamy coffee.

Sarah, just fifteen, sat in the cold train station weeping. She didn't look up as a female recruiter, a former Madame employee with a keen eye for spotting potential girls spoke to her.

"Do you need help, dear?" the former soiled dove asked her. She could see the girl was likely a runaway. Abused by her uncle, Sarah had left home and had been living at the station when the 'kind lady' promised a warm bed and hot meals. Not too bright-it took a couple of days before

Sarah figured out what a 'warm bed' meant-she couldn't stop crying.

"Sarah, you have got to stop that weeping," Madame told her one day in her office. "I can't send my clients to a girl whose eyes are puffy every night." Sarah sobbed even harder and eventually found herself back on the street.

Caught

Martha Webster noticed David's visits were longer than at the beginning of the tailoring projects. It riled her to think the wealthy man might be getting free services right under her nose.

Etta heard footsteps on the back stairs early one September day while resting after love-making with David.

"Listen! Hide! whispered Etta. David quickly jumped up and hid behind the nearby screen. Etta pushed down her skirt, grabbed his clothes, and shoved them under the cot just as Madame entered the room. She had come down to have Etta fix a loose button on her jacket.

"Good gracious, Etta, what are you doing on the floor, pray tell? And your bed is un-made. And why is that? It's 'way past noon."

Not knowing what to reply, Etta said the first thing that came to her mind. "Uh, I've lost my slipper." Even to Etta, her reason for being on the floor sounded flimsy.

"Oh, really? Lost your slipper. My, my, how unfortunate," Madame responded, her tone sarcastic. Looking around, she spotted David's pocket watch and cuff links on the sewing table. Ah, now I remember. Mr. Andrews had afitting with Etta that morning. She looked over at the screen, where David hid, naked, bent over with his hands over his mouth, trying to suppress his laughter. Madame said nothing and headed for the stairs, adding, "Well, I hope you find your slipper." Now she had to decide what to do about this problem. I may have to change my plans for Etta, she thought.

Moving Upstairs

Madame sat at her desk staring out the dreary window. The dressmaking field had narrowed, as the girls could pick out a gown from one of the new department stores and wear it that night. Moving Etta upstairs would be the transition to her career change and do away with the nonsense of David Andrews' unpaid visits to the bordello. Etta could begin bringing in real income.

Etta also knew that the stores narrowed the field of dressmaking.

The day after discovering the liaison, Madame sent Molly to the sewing room. Etta was busy picking a lace for Sadie's new spring gown and hated the interruption.

"Miss Etta, Madame wants to see you."

What is going on? She had been so careful to do her work and stay pleasant to Madame. She trod up the stairs, her apprehension increasing with each step.

"You wanted to see me?" she asked Madame.

"Yes, please sit down."

Warning bells resounded in Etta's mind when she heard

those words. People heard them when they were about to be fired from the tailor or when a husband wanted a divorce.

"How have you been, Henrietta-do you like it here?" Asked Martha dryly. Her demeanor held little of her usual warmth or friendliness. Not looking at her employee, she shuffled papers on her desk as she spoke.

"Yes, I'm quite happy here, thank you, Madame." Why have I been summoned, she wondered.

"Well, you'll be pleased to know I am moving you to a front bedroom on the second floor."

Etta froze. An icy hand grabbed her heart. Madame reserved those rooms for the most experienced girls whose clients were the wealthiest men. So it is happening. I will now make my living on my back instead of with my hands.

"You will be moving this afternoon, Henrietta. I'll send Arthur down to help you with your things. Good afternoon." With that, she rose and bid Etta goodbye.

As though in a dream, Etta slowly made her way back down the stairs. She hated sleeping on that cot in the sewing room with its dampness and constant chill. But now, the little room in the basement seemed more like home than ever to her.

On Edge

The cloud of perfume sprayed throughout the halls every night hung in the air and followed Etta to her new bedroom like an old memory.

She stood at the door and looked around. Luxurious furniture, damask drapes, and huge oil paintings sat silently before her. Why this sudden change from her employer? It wasn't just the move-Madame seemed cooler, more distant to Etta. Did she see us together yesterday in the sewing room? I doubt it, she thought.

She began putting her meager belongings away in the wardrobe. She picked up the kitten-called 'Blanc" since Etta had started French lessons-and nuzzled her against her cheek as she got her pet situated in the private bathroom. She moved slowly, preoccupied with what would be happening to her body the next night.

Sitting by the tall window after settling in, she thought, the view is the same, but now I see tops of heads and people in carriages, not feet. And I'm sure it's more than my perspective that will be changing. She pondered her situation. A meeting with David was scheduled in a few days. She shook her head and tried to push away the dread from her mind. She began twirling her hair. Am I going to be put to work up here? What will I tell David? How will he react to this change?

The Doctor Returns

Madame didn't waste any time. The following day Etta had a visitor the before she could dress properly. "Yes?" she called.

"Good Morning, Mrs. King," greeted the doctor as he set down his bag. She recognized him as the physician she had seen her first day at the bordello.

"Good morning, Doctor Thorne. What is it? I'm not ill."

"Mrs. Webster wanted me to check you over now that you are living upstairs."

Etta's stomach dropped.

"Please remove your nightdress and lie down," the doctor ordered.

The examination did not begin at her head this time.

"Have you recently experienced sexual activity?" queried the doctor.

Etta knew better than to lie.

"Uh," she cleared her throat. "Well-yes."

"I see," replied the doctor. "And your last menses?"

Etta felt rattled. "I'm not sure, Doctor, uh, I guess a couple of weeks ago."

The physician lectured her about sexually transmitted diseases, proper hygiene, and birth control." If you become pregnant, please do inform Mrs. Webster immediately," he added and left.

On the first day upstairs at the bordello, leaden dread fell on her like a shroud, tightening every hour.

How am I ever going to get out of this, she worried as she dressed. What is it going to be like? How will I react? Can I prevent showing my disgust? How am I going to deal with the shame? She looked at her reflection in the gold-leafed mirror and whispered, "Please, God, no. Please. No."

Headed West

After church service the next day, David's father, James, announced, "Son, I have a proposition for you." He and his oldest son were strolling along the shimmering blue lake. James's wife and other children were away for the summer.

"There's some land out Colorado way I'd like you to look at with me. There might be some mining opportunities on the property."

This proposal put off David. He knew it would be a long trip. He had several irons in the fire regarding his own real estate dealings. And, too, this trip would mean he couldn't be with Etta.

His father stopped and stared at him, waiting for a reply. David knew he couldn't say 'no', and perhaps being alone for a couple of weeks would shrink the distance between him and his father since their move to Chicago a few years before.

"Yes, Father, of course. When would you like to leave?"

"I have tickets for the morning train to Denver." His

father flicked his cigar ashes on the sidewalk without looking up and continued his stroll.

David, livid, turned his head toward the boats gliding on the lake so James wouldn't notice his anger.

"Yes, Father. Well, guess I'd better get home and pack." David said with a forced smile.

His father didn't reply. He didn't care to hear anything David had to say.

Denver

David stared out the train window as the farmlands grew into mountains. The more miles distanced David from his love, the more his mind drifted back to her scent and soft skin. He hadn't told his father about her—he didn't dare. James would undoubtedly cut him out of his will if he knew the girl he loved worked in the shady neighborhood where the crime bred only more crime. James would never believe Etta worked as a dressmaker. Gossip around the bordello was rarely definitive. The Levee District was the Levee District, and everyone knew its reputation.

David hadn't been able to talk to Etta before his departure; he barely had time to send her a note by courier telling her of his plans.

In Denver, the father and son checked into a tavern. While enjoying thick western steaks, a man passed by, stopped, turned, and approached their table.

"James Andrews, how good to see you. What are you doing so far from home?"

Hiram Swell, a former business crony of James', had worked with him several times on real estate transactions in the West. He looked more tan and weathered than the last time James had seen him, most likely from living the Western outdoor life.

James stood and introduced his son.

"Nice to meet you, David, I've heard a lot about you. You attended college in Ohio, as I recall."

David rose and shook the man's hand. "Yes, sir, Mr. Swell, but now I am working with my father and Uncle Matthew."

"Good for you, David. You are in the right business. Lots of potential markets in this great land. . . more people and opportunities are arriving every day."

The trio met later in the saloon to catch up on the latest news and trends in the land speculation business.

"What are you here for, James?" Hiram asked. "Care to share?"

"I heard about a parcel up in the mountains that may hold some possibilities for mining. But you know I'm not going to tell you where it is," he laughed.

"How's the rest of the family?" said Hiram.

"Thanks for asking," James replied. "Nancy is busy with her charity work and our oldest son, Peter is at medical school at Yale. The next one is studying architecture, and the youngest plans to start law school in a couple of years."

"And the girls?"

"The oldest is still at Bryn Mawr—our youngest will start Smith next fall. We had them close together, which hit my wallet pretty hard, but you know, we never think about those things at the time." James said with a smirk.

A Heart Attack

The crisp Colorado mountain air invigorated father and son as they rode on horseback on an old Indian trail up the mountain to the Cripple Creek Mining District.

"I'd forgotten what fresh air smells like," Jim yelled at his son, trailing behind. "Makes me want to move out here."

David offered no response, too busy reveling in the stunning scenery and the joy of being astride again.

Suddenly David saw his father lurch in his saddle and clutch his chest, his eyes as big as the Western sky. He grabbed the saddle horn and slid to the side, catching one foot in his stirrup as he fell. The horse whinnied, skittering sideways, dragging James's shoulder along the rocks. David jumped down from his mount and ran to his father, who gasped for air.

"Oh no! Father!" David cried. "Father!"

The guide quickly dismounted and ran back to help. "I think he's having a heart attack," shouted the guide. "We've got to get him back down quick." The guide, familiar with this reaction that some older clients had at the high altitudes, helped David hoist his father on the back of his mount and race back down the mountain. The only sounds were the horses' steamy breaths and t h e i r hooves clattering on the stony path. They arrived at the hospital in less than a half-hour and dragged Jim inside.

"Help, please!" David shouted to anyone within ear.

Hours passed. The doctor came out to the waiting room. "Mr. Andrews?"

David jumped up. "Yes?" He realized he had been holding his breath from the moment the doctor entered.

"Your father is going to make it, but we'll have to keep him a few days."

The opposing feelings of joy and dread tore through David's psyche—delight at the news and worry at being away from Etta any longer. He sent her a wire telling her of the delay.

The Murder

That same night in Chicago, the fall wind howled, attacking the city with more savage energy than usual. Etta had worked late as she still had much to finish before the Christmas Ball, still weeks away. She sat by her large window sewing on covered buttons as darkness enveloped the bordello, trying not to think about what she would be doing the next night. Her body felt as tense as a high-wire walker.

The hall suddenly resounded with a deafening scream from Grace's room. Some of the clients and scantily garbed girls hurriedly rushed into the hall. Grace stood at her door, her naked body covered in blood. A glint from the hall gas light revealed the knife in her hand. " He's dead. I've killed him," she cried, falling to her knees.

Covering her with a robe, Katie rushed over and led her toward the empty room, 'sobbing Sarah' had just vacated. By that time, Madame and Arthur had arrived. Madame pushed the crowd aside and led Grace into the room.

Madame nodded toward Grace's room at Arthur. "Go see what happened," she told him. She turned and faced the gaping half-dressed group that had gathered. "The rest of you, get back to your business. Now!"

Although Etta stood the farthest away at her room at the front of the building, she could still see and hear the scene down the hall. "Oh, God, help her," she whispered.

Madame helped the hysterical girl onto the chaise and sat beside her, her arm around her. "Now, now, Grace, try to calm down and tell me what happened."

After several body-wracking sobs, Grace spoke. "He wanted me to do something dreadful," she moaned. "And when I said 'no' he threatened to cut my face and scar me for life. I managed to get the knife away from him when he rolled over."

Madame's silence calmed the girl. This is serious, indeed, she thought.

Arthur knocked on the door.

"Come in."

Arthur shook his head.

Grace burst into hysterical sobs again. Madame tried to soothe her. "Arthur, go get something to help this poor girl," she instructed.

The butler knew what she meant-opium.

"And then send for the Chief."

The police chief shook his head as he sat across from Martha. "I'm afraid there's no way I can minimize this, Martha," he said. "The victim's family is too well-known for me to be able to interfere with the investigation in any way."

"Thank you, Chief," Martha said. The publicity is going to be a nightmare, she thought.

Reprieve

Gossip buzzed through the bordello like thirsty mosquitoes in May. Madame called a meeting of the staff first thing the following day.

"This gossip has got to stop," directed Madame. "There's enough talk going around the city about that poor dead boy without my own house adding to it. You will refrain from discussing the incident. If you wish, I will give you daily updates about Grace's condition at the jail and any new developments. Does everyone understand me?"

Heads bobbed up and down, but most were looking at the floor. The twins were whispering to one another. Madame glowered at them.

Police examined Grace's room and interviewed the girls at the bordello.

Meanwhile, the newspapers went berserk. A prosecutor arraigned Grace, and the court scheduled a preliminary hearing. Life at the bordello had turned upside-down.

Luckily for Etta, Martha Webster became utterly consumed by the case. Her plans for the seamstress dissipated like morning dew.

Etta realized that when Madame had not contacted her over the next few weeks. She kept a low profile by hiding in her new room. The other girls thought she continued her dressmaking duties and never questioned her move.

Etta felt relief surge through her as she realized she had been granted yet another reprieve from her cruel fate—first, her illness at arriving at the bordello, then reassignment as a dressmaker, and now, the murder. She felt like a cat being given another life. Thank You, God. I'm so sorry this had to happen to Grace, but thank you. Thank you.

Turned Away

Back in Chicago a few days later, after David read his mail and the newspapers that had piled up outside his suite door, he rushed to the bordello and gave the usual knock to inform Arthur of an off-hours visitor. As he waited, David watched the stable manager, Richard, chase a young barefoot boot polisher lad off the premises.

Arthur opened the door but did not step back to allow David inside.

"Yes?" Arthur said.

Arthur's behavior puzzled David. "Arthur, it's me, Mr. Andrews."

"Yes, Sir?" asked Arthur once again.

"I'm here to see Mrs. King—to pick up my new suit." Arthur could see the puzzlement on David's face.

"Yes, Sir, I understand. I've been given instructions by Mrs. Webster to tell you your suit will be delivered to your hotel." With that, he began closing the door.

David wedged his foot in the jamb. "Arthur. Wait. I need to talk to Mrs. Webster. Immediately." David's tone reflected impatience, accustomed as he was to having his orders followed by servants.

"Sorry, Mrs. Webster is in a meeting right now. I will let her know you would like to see her." The door closed.

David stood on the stoop. What just happened? What is going on?

Together Again

David had read about the murder in *The Tribune*. He needed to talk to Etta but could only reach her by courier. He had to see her; he wrote her asking her to meet at his suite at the Palmer House the following day.

Etta flung herself into his arms. "I've missed you so much," she cried, holding him close.

His mouth followed the line of her hair as he murmured, "Darling, not nearly as much as I've missed you." He covered her face and neck with kisses, backing her toward the large walnut bed in his suite. Uncle Matthew was out of town in Virginia to tend to family business, so he and Etta would be alone.

"Oh, God, how I have missed this," he exclaimed, unlacing her bodice. Trembling with passion, as often now happened with her lover, Etta moaned as his lips explored her white body, taking his time to awaken every nerve.

She later caught him up on the latest news of the murder at the bordello. "Poor girl, it looks as though she is going to plead guilty, but killed him to save herself from becoming disfigured." The gruesome details of the murder dominated the news.

"What an awful thing for you to witness," David murmured. "How are you?"

"Horrible, as well you can guess," Etta replied, staring at the oriental rug on the floor. "No one should have to ever see something like that. I can't get the image out of my mind. That poor girl. I can't imagine what she is going through right now in that horrid jail. But it may have provided a reprieve for me."

Before David could ask her what she meant, a knock pierced the somber mood of the room.

"Yes?" David called. The couple still needed to be fully dressed.

"Mr. Andrews?"

"Yes?" David asked again, with some impatience.

"Your lunch, Sir." A voice answered.

"Oh," David whispered, "I nearly forgot."

The couple dressed and began enjoying their meal.

"How is your father doing?"

"Thank you for asking—he's better, but will never fully recover. "He's already turned some of his dealings over to me. My step-mother Nancy is devastated, of course, and came straight home from summering in Canada to care for him."

Anxious to ask Etta about the move upstairs—had she been required to service men, or had she been able to keep her dressmaking tasks? He decided there may be better times to ask. And do I really want to know?

After the Parade

A few days later, Etta, sitting on the edge of her satin-covered bed, bent down to unlace her high-buttoned red patent leather shoes. "I'm pregnant!" she whispered, gently touching her stomach. "And I'm going to become Mrs. David Andrews!"

The annual fall parade provided a welcome distraction from the chaos swirling around the house after the murder. Madame decided to allow the girls' participation to bring some semblance of normalcy into their lives and attempt to improve the deteriorating reputation of the house.

All the bordellos in the Levee District displayed their feminine wares in an annual parade. The girls rode in carriages bursting with finery; the drivers wore formal suits and tall silk hats. As they proceeded down the parade route lined with thousands of onlookers, the girls threw kisses and flowers to the crowd. The myriad colors made the parade look like a summery rainbow winding through the masses. Church ladies marched alongside with signs that warned of Hell, damnation, or safe places to go if the 'soiled doves' ever wished to leave the profession.

A lottery decided the carriage order in the parade, as no one wanted a repeat of the shooting in the past about which carriage should go first. Chicago seemed to be working hard to earn its reputation as the roughest gateway to the West.

Etta struggled out of her scarlet taffeta gown, dark circles under the arms from the day's oppressive heat. She couldn't wait to immerse herself in an aromatic bath and lather away the city smells. The day had been roasting for October, and the clip-clop of the harnessed teams' hooves still rang in her ears.

Etta rang for Molly to draw her bath and help her unlace her corset. While she waited, she recalled how her life would change. How was she going to tell him? Was the wealthy family of her lover going to accept her? They were all in the social 'Blue Book,' as was David. Did his family even know about her? Etta wondered. Or was her identity hidden in whispers behind gloved hands? Where would the wedding be? Would his family attend? Where would she and David live? Could they move into the gorgeous mansion in the Lake District with David's family? The excitement fluttered in her stomach like a trapped butterfly.

She thought about her mother-Mary Claire-when she was pregnant with Etta. Also unmarried, but an unplanned conception at that time. How could she walk out after my birth, not looking back, never to be heard from again--vanishing--like drying tears on a baby's face?

She couldn't wait to tell David. They had a date for dinner at the Palmer House that evening, October 11, 1877. She rang again for Molly. The little maid, all chatter, wanted to know everything about the parade, but Etta found herself in the mood to be pensive and alone.

The Walk Home

The clock struck eight as David delivered Etta to the bordello after the couple's dinner at the Palmer House Hotel that October evening.

Cold as it was, David decided to walk the short blocks back to his hotel. He needed to clear his head, going over the conversation repeatedly as doubt spread its black hood over his thoughts.

A lone carriage rattled by as he approached the hotel. He stopped, turned, and headed down to the lake. Lost in his thoughts, he never felt the cold gust of wind slam him, nearly taking his hat—he was so preoccupied with the problem.

She is pregnant. But with whose child? I suppose it could it be mine. Perhaps—we have been together for several months. I assumed she was taking precautions. That was a mistake—I've been a lovesick fool.

David knew he could never prove he didn't father the child. He had to take Etta's word. *Yes, we've been lovers, but she told me Madame had moved her upstairs at the bordello while I was in Denver. Had she then begun her life* as a soiled dove? I returned ten days later. I can't bring myself to ask her—I just can't, he thought. It would be the end of me–my business, my social standing. He imagined polite society looking down with haughty disdain at the couple's union through their jeweled lorgnettes.

The snow had stopped, and the moon spread wavy white ribbons over the lake, mirroring the Milky Way sparkling overhead on the clear, chilly night.

Morally, David knew what to do. He had to take responsibility. He had to pay. It was his duty. But marry her? Never.

The newly rich in the mid-western city had to reach farther back into their family heritages for blue blood, success, and sterling reputations. The gold and glitz added to nearly all the new Chicago buildings reflected society's desire to 'run with the big boys' of New York and Paris. David's family was no different. The cloud of shame of a marriage out of their blue-blood circles would not be allowed to permeate the refined air of their gilded mansions or intimate gatherings.

David recognized that his life had taken a sharp turn on this day. From this night forward, his life would be measured in 'before this night' and 'after this night'.

He turned with a jerk and headed back toward the hotel. He needed a drink.

Rejection

Later that October night after the Palmer House dinner, Etta lay awake for hours, twirling her hair and repeatedly going over the conversation. She punched herself. What was I thinking? She knew David would never marry a trades-person, especially one working in the Levee District, no matter how much in love with her he had been. I must have been demented. She put her face on her pillow and wept. Now, indeed, she found herself in a pickle. Her thoughts rustled around her head like scurrying mice in a cupboard.

She looked at her swollen eyes the following day and decided not to join the others for breakfast. She didn't feel up to facing them.

But David had offered a caveat the night before. "Well, here is what I am willing to do." He cleared his throat and added a silver teaspoonful of sugar to his coffee. "I'll be willing to rent a small place where you can board. And of course, I will take care of the upkeep of you and your child."

Small consolation, she thought the following day, after she had dreamt of becoming Mrs. David Andrews and a respected member of Chicago society, but better than being on the streets or getting an abortion. But the disappointment pressed against her like a broken stay, sharp and painful.

She crept over to Katie's room and knocked on the door. "Can I talk to you?" she whispered.

Katie opened the door. "Hi, how are ya'! Come in! Lord, let me tell you about the fellah I had last night!" Since she was near-sighted, she hadn't noticed Etta's swollen and reddened eyes. "Have a seat, girl!" Katie frequently reverted to her 'country way' of talking when not working.

Katie then noticed her friend's face. "What is it? What's going on?" She put her arm around Etta's shoulders and led her to a chair.

Etta told her the whole story, breaking down, sobbing halfway through.

"Etta, look," Katie said, grabbing her shoulders. "You ain't lookin' at this the right way."

Etta looked up at her through her tears.

She took Etta's face in her hands. "Now you listen to me. You just need to change your attitude. You're nearly getting it all!" She went on. "Think about it, honey, he just may marry you after that crazy old daddy of his kicks the bucket. Didn't he just have a heart attack? That's the way you need be thinking."

Etta thought about what her friend had said. It would help if she changed her viewpoint. She sat up straight and sighed. "You may be right, Katie." She paused for a moment. "It's going to be hard, but I'm going to try."

"Try, my ass!" Katie yelled. She looked around to see if anyone had heard her swearing. "You gotta survive, girl No man wants a sad-faced bleary-eyed girl wandering around feeling sorry for herself, and with a bulging belly to boot.

Now you just go out there and put on a pretty face for him. So you didn't get exactly what you wanted, but you gonna get a good bit of it."

By supper, Etta had pulled herself together. She began to feel more optimistic, envisioning her daily life with David, even though they wouldn't be married. She imagined him coming home to dinner every evening, having coffee in the parlor, going to bed at night, knowing his face would be the first thing she saw every morning.

She envisioned taking baby David to the park, their baby cooing at the passers-by, snuggling in her arms while she snuggled in David's. The birthday parties—would she have new friends? she wondered. Where would little David be christened? Would the family attend? Or would they shun and shame her? When she would catch herself having these thoughts, she would give herself a quick pinch, shake her head, and resolve to stop. I'm going to have a new beginning. That's what I need to concentrate on.

She thought about life with just the three of them. The more she fabricated these domestic scenes, the more excited she became. Who cares if we aren't married? Most people took that bond for granted when a couple lived together.

Today presented a new life.

The Fog

Something nudged her consciousness. Utter quiet greeted her. She rolled over, trying to pull herself up from the dark embrace of sleep. She heard the clock downstairs chime the quarter—a quarter of what? She felt wide awake, sat up, rubbed her eyes, and put on her robe and slippers. Chilled by the early hour, she pulled her robe more tightly around her and walked over to the tall window.

She couldn't see a thing outside. The horse's hooves pulling the lone carriage on the street below sounded deafening yet eerily hollow. Probably the milk truck, she thought—it may be light soon.

Curious, she opened the window—nothing but white outside. It felt to her like being inside a bale of cotton. A rush of smells surrounded her—holding her in their ugly embrace. She slammed the casement shut, but the odor stayed with her—clinging to her robe and hair.

She reached for her perfume bottle, sprayed the room, and sat down. The house was silent. She had never seen fog that thick in Chicago. And the stench reminded her of

Pittsburgh. Immediately a feeling of depression overcame her.

Was it just last night that David told her he could never marry her? Then she remembered the conversation with Katie. I have to change my thinking. Etta gently put her hand on her stomach. In only a few weeks, she would leave this life into which fate had dragged her just a year ago. She now had an opportunity to walk away and never look back. It certainly wasn't exactly her vision, but at least the bordello would be left behind. And she and David would be together.

What should I take? I won't need much. Will I have any occasion to wear the silks and satins I wore for special events? I can't wear them with a big belly. I wonder if David will buy me new clothes? Clothes that make me look like an ordinary girl shopping for the best cut of veal. Clothes that make me feel like a wife.

Telling Madame

She had to tell Madame. With a mix of dread and joy, she approached her office and knocked on the door.

"Yes, Etta? What is it? Please, sit down. Is everything all right?" She suddenly remembered wanting to put the girl to work on the second floor and realized she had been so engrossed with Grace's upcoming trial she had utterly forgotten about her. I've got to get that girl to work, she thought. Every day she isn't working looses income for my bordello.

Etta sat down. "Um, Madame, um..."

"Well?" Madame said impatiently. "What is it?"

"I'm going to be leaving, Madame. I'm pregnant." Etta didn't look up. Her fingers were nervously playing with a loose thread she had found on her dress.

Madame felt stunned. Then, she remembered the day she caught Etta on the floor just a few weeks ago by her cot, David's cuff links on the table. Ah, she thought. I was right about him—sneaking free ones right under my nose. She felt a stab of anger in her chest. And I was so good to him, letting him access my dressmaker. Men!

Etta wondered why Madame wasn't saying anything — just staring at her, which made her even more nervous.

Madame rose. "Well, fine. I will deliver a bill of what you owe me for medical bills, room, and board." And out she marched.

Fury overtook Etta. How about all the thousands of hours I had toiled over those damned dresses? She had been paid a little but imagined colossal expenses for all the classes, room, and board she had received while in Madame's employ. She rose, turned, and stomped out of the office.

Molly passed her in the parlor. "Hey, Miss Etta, you all right?" She could see how angry she was.

"Leave me alone!" barked Etta and marched up the stairs.

David paid her bill in full.

The Move

The trees were bare, and the morning cold when Etta packed her things and told the girls goodbye. Her corset, hooked more loosely, felt tighter. Just before her departure, she visited Katie's room. "Here, Katie, I don't think I'll be needing these any longer," and she gave her her two best dresses, the red satin worn the parade day she realized she was pregnant and the beaded green velvet worn the night David learned about the baby at the Palmer House.

"You'll look beautiful in them," she told Katie. "You can wear the green to the First Ward Ball," They hugged and promised to meet often.

"I'll come see you, Katie," Etta cried as she hugged her. "I'll only be a few blocks away."

But she knew she was leaving this life in the Levee district behind forever. I'll never come back, not to visit, not for birthdays, parties, not ever. I'm locking this door and throwing away the key forever.

***

The new house-one of the few in that neighborhood-had escaped the fire of 1871. Ample for one person-with a parlor in front, dining room, kitchen, and a small bedroom o to the side-it had been vracated by a client of David's, now seeking his fortune in the West.

David helped Etta settle in, filled the kitten's water bowl, and kissed her goodbye.

"I'll be back this evening, Love," he smiled at her. "And I'll get you some books from the library."

David enjoyed the manners, speech, and decorum Etta had learned at Martha Webster's but still thought her horizons needed broadening. He would bring her *Crime and Punishment*, *War and Peace*, and *Anna Karenina* from Chicago's public library.

Etta bent over the toilet bowl with morning sickness for weeks. Daily sessions with the white porcelain mouth often made her wonder if she had made the right decision. The silence in her new home sounded as deafening as the trains that used to pass her room in the rear of the bordello. She sat by her parlor window and watched the goings-on at the park across the street as children skated, rolled hoops, and had snowball fights. Their mothers and nannies sat on benches, hats and feathers bobbing like mating prairie grouse, exchanging the day's gossip.

Etta sighed and put her book down. She picked up Blanc and began reminiscing about her life at the bordello, wondering what the girls were doing. I enjoyed fine meals and clothes there. Plays, museums, and concerts were part of my everyday life. Now she just read the ads and reviews in the papers for the latest popular cultural events and tried to recall how it felt to sit in the darkness of a theater flying into another reality. Her only companions now were Tolstoy and Dostoevsky unless the grocery boy rang the bell or the cleaning woman came to chase dust motes and cat hair. David stopped by two or three days a week, but his visits grew less as her belly grew.

The pain of missing her father and siblings returned. But if her family in Pennsylvania visited, how could she explain her pregnancy? They thought her 'husband', Charles King, had passed away over a year ago.

1877 was a dark, drab, and dreary winter in Chicago. The early snows increased along with Etta's waist. Lethargy moved in, and some days, Etta didn't get out of bed.

She was talking to Blanc when, one morning, she felt a flutter in her belly, like the little sulfur butterfly she had admired that long-ago day along the Monongahela River in Pittsburgh. "Blanc, here-the baby is kicking! Want to feel it?" Or, she would exclaim, "I hate Dostoevsky. Do you hate Dostoevsky, Blanc? I REALLY hate Dostoevski." She pronounced his name 'Dovesky.' The cat looked at her blankly, then dutifully began licking herself.

Etta sighed and began to plan what she would make for dinner out of sheer boredom. She wanted a healthy baby and had learned to cook in Pittsburgh as a working girl. She loved cooking 'Mulligan stew', which involved throwing all the leftovers in the icebox into a pot, adding tomatoes, an onion, spices, parsley, and perhaps a leftover piece of meat.

She hated eating alone. She began letting Blanc sit on the table with her while she ate. Sometimes the cat would put a white paw in the bowl, turning it red, other times she turning up her nose and jumping down, tail in the air as though snubbing 'people food'.

Christmas Eve

Winter claimed normal life in Chicago. One of the worst snowstorms of the century had brought the great city to its knees, burying everything in silent white and swallowing the shoreline. The only sounds outdoors were the scrapes of the men's shovels cleaning the streets and the huffing of the horses hauling the snow away in wagons.

* * *

One freezing February day, memories of a long-ago Christmas Eve when she was thirteen struck Etta like an unexpected slap. She recalled visiting her papa and his family in Pennsylvania.

"How are you doing, Etta," her papa asked, his hand on her shoulder as the snow crunched beneath their feet. "Are the Gellers treating you right?"

Etta thought about the couple under whose care she lived in Pittsburgh.

"Yes, Papa. They're very good to me. Mrs. Geller is a wonderful wife and mother."

"Well, that's a relief. After your nana died, I wasn't sure when my sister up there in Indiana County told me about the Gellers. I only had her word to go on. I was purdy worried."

She looked down and smiled at the country way he said, 'purdy.' She had learned to speak in a more educated way since she was now a 'city girl' living in Pittsburgh. She grabbed his hand and squeezed it. "I've missed these walks with you so much." The pair followed the steam from their breath down the road.

After a long silence, she asked him to tell her more stories about the war. Had he served in Gettysburg? Or Bull Run? She'd been studying the war in school.

"No, Darlin,' neither of those, but I did fight at Cold Harbor, Petersburg, and Appomattox."

Etta had never heard of those and pouted in disappointment. "Where were those places?"

"Well," they continued strolling along the snowy road, enjoying the white vista around them. "Virginee, uh, let's see... Maryland, mostly around them places."

"Did you shoot anybody, Papa? Did you kill any of those Rebs?"

"Well, Etta, that's a question I can't answer. Those boys were purdy far away. I did see some fall down after I shot, but I would hate to think that I took a life."

"But why, Papa—they were bad men."

"No, Darlin', not bad–jes' young boys, fightin' for what they was taught to believe in, same as us."

Etta fell silent. So much to think about.

"Did any of your friends die, Papa?"

Her papa continued walking, head down. He didn't answer right away. "Some, I reckon."

The cry of crows pierced the cold air, and the sky darkened.

"You've seen everything, Papa!" Etta jumped up and down. "Someday I want to see the world, too!"

"Well, you've been to Pittsburgh!" he laughed, their heads touching. "And I'm sure you'll get around a bit as you get older. You got plenty of time. Just keep your eyes out for opportunities, and you know I'll always be there for you. Just write me if you need anything."

* * *

Etta reached down, picked up Blanc, and stroked her fur. When the sleigh bells and laughter filtered through the window, tears began to flow. She missed her Papa so much —his voice, smell, hugs, and, mostly, boundless love.

Blanc jumped down and began chasing her tail.

The Holidays

David stopped by to visit Etta Christmas morning after church services with his family. He had skipped their traditional family Christmas breakfast, claiming he already had an invitation. They didn't inquire with whom.

He arrived brimming with Christmas cheer as he embraced and kissed his love soundly. He had brought lavish gifts–an alpaca stole, a new china plate to paint, a bottle of 'Milles Fleurs' perfume, soft slippers, white stockings, and a box of candies from Thompson Chocolates, Etta's favorite.

David loved his gold Cross pen and silently wondered how she purchased it. Perhaps Mrs. Parker...

Temporary contentment crept into Etta's life whenever David came around.

She survived New Year's Eve by going to bed at eight, even though the levity on the streets awoke her at midnight. She rolled over, cuddled Blanc, and went back to sleep, trying to block out thoughts of what her friends were doing and the joy and festivity swirling about her.

The new year was 1878, the year Etta's child would be born. Her son. Her little David. She hoped he would have his father's dark eyes and sweet disposition, and she would be a good mother. She hoped the baby would be healthy. She hoped—and hoped—and hoped.

But this day felt different. This New Year's Day was, in every sector, country, and decade, a day of promise, hope, and a new beginning for every soul on the earth.

David had the usual New Year's Day breakfast with his cronies at the Union League Club, then began his obligatory annual visitations. Engraved calling cards in hand, he looked at his list, then started his tour, leaving his card in the porch baskets of friends who had fled winter's blast for the south. He stayed the obligatory twenty minutes for those at home receiving guests, leaving his card in the sterling trays in the foyers. New Year's Day duties accomplished, he set out for Etta's.

"Happy New Year, Dear," David greeted her as she answered his knock. He never used his key as he didn't want nosy neighbors to notice that he had more than a passing interest in the house's occupant. He tried to look like a visitor, a landlord.

Etta grabbed him, sobbing.

"What is it, Darling?"

Etta looked at him as though she couldn't believe he didn't know what bothered her. Part of her wished he didn't believe her and inquired further, but he appeared ignorant to her despair. But how could he possibly? He probably hadn't spent a day alone in his entire life and could never understand the depression and loneliness she experienced through the holidays. No point in burdening him with her troubles.

"Oh, nothing, Dear. Just missing everyone." She choked back a sob. "Happy New Year. Would you like a brandy?"

David smiled. He nodded, sat down, and lit a cigar as he finished a slice of the nougat almond cake Etta had baked for him. He was in heaven: his love, a fine brandy, and a Cuban cigar. All was well in David's world.

The Escape

One unusually warm day in January, Etta decided to escape from the house. A visit to Madam Vertina was in order. She dressed hurriedly, changing three times until she could find a dress that fit, slipped on a light-weight roomy coat, grabbed her handbag, and set out for the fortune teller.

The seer was surprised to see her. "You're in luck my girl; I don't have other appointments at this time, next time send note requesting a time."

Etta explained her situation even though the seer could see the apparent problem Etta had created for herself.

She explained how David refused to marry her, his restrictions, her loneliness, and depression.

"I have potion." Madam calmed Etta down. "Will help, make you feel better."

She disappeared into her kitchen. After a few moments, she returned with a large steamy cup of amber liquid. It smelled strange, but Etta's trust in the fortune teller was so complete that she accepted it. The tea consisted of chamomile, St. John's Wort, and clover honey. Etta felt a warmth take over her body as the room brightened.

"I give you take home." Madam produced a box of loose tea. "Only two dollar a pound." Etta jumped at the chance to escape the choking, debilitation fog of sadness that had taken over her life but was struck by the high price. Etta thought for a minute. That is a lot of money. She usually paid about sixty cents a pound for green tea.

"And this," Madam went on. She brought a beautiful pendant of polished tourmaline stone set in a gold pendant and chain. "Only fifteen dollar."

Although David quietly filled the coffee jar in Etta's kitchen with cash regularly, she wasn't sure she had enough to pay for it. "Can I bring the rest next time?" she asked.

"Of course." The seer put the pendant aside. Too many city people were dying of cholera and diphtheria for her to hand anything over before being paid.

Etta's steps were lighter as she shuffled the short block to the cars. She felt better already. She had faith in the potion. She was sure the cloud would lift and her time would fly.

Admonition

She stood, expecting a hug and kiss from David as he placed his hat and coat on the settee without looking at her, which was not a good sign. A warning bell clanged in Etta's mind.

"What is it, Dear? Has something happened?" She wanted to run over to him, embrace him, and smother him with kisses but knew instinctively to stay where she was.

"Sit down, Etta." David commanded.

Etta plopped down on the easy chair, eyes wide. David did not sit, towering over her as he stood just a few inches away.

"What is it?" Etta repeated, a large lump in her throat. Not many options remained for her if something went wrong with their relationship. Five months pregnant, unmarried. She had a fleeting thought of running to her father's house.

"Etta, Mrs. Parker came by last week. And you weren't home."

Etta froze. She had forgotten the cleaning woman was due Wednesday, the day she escaped to the fortune teller.

She was not supposed to go out; if David knew about the seer, things would go badly. She hadn't planned an excuse for this transgression.

She needed to buy some time to think and struggled up, her belly making the move difficult. "Oh, Darling, I've left a kettle of water on the stove. I'll be right back. Do you want anything? Tea? Coffee?"

David merely stared at her, which unnerved her even more. Panic began rising in her chest like a tiny bubbling volcano.

Etta pushed Blanc off the kitchen table and turned on the gas in the kitchen. No! Off, not on! David will hear the hiss. She quickly turned it off and poured most of the cold water out of the kettle. Standing by the stove, she thought, what should I say? Tell the truth?

Etta returned, cold cup of tea in hand. "David, Dear, I'm sure you will understand. It was such a beautiful day, and the park so alluring, that I just stepped out for an hour." She swallowed and cleared her throat, then looked up at him innocently. "I'm sure you understand," she repeated.

David just looked at her, trying to decide whether or not to believe her.

"It was such a lovely day..." she went on falteringly. She waited and rubbed her ballooning stomach, feeling the dance of tiny feet. She took David's hand and placed it on her belly. "Here—feel—your son is saying, 'hello, Daddy'."

The Machine

Etta had wiped up the last remnants of lunch when she heard a knock at the door. A man in a uniform stood on the stoop. "Yes?" Etta inquired.

"Hello, Misses. I'm from the Sound Telegraph Company, here to install the machine in your house."

Etta was confused. What machine? Who sent him?

Seeing her quizzical look, he took a pad out of his pocket and read it. "A Mister Andrews sent me, ma'am. He needs to be able to talk to you whenever. . ." He stopped, looking at her ballooning stomach, and cleared his throat. "When the time comes." He shuffled his feet, looking away at the park across the street.

Suspicious about letting this stranger in her house when alone, Etta hesitated. "What kind of machine?"

"It's a talking machine, ma'am. You can call Mr. Andrews any time you want to, and can talk to him on it."

"What?" Etta had never heard of such a thing. "How?" she asked, trying to stall.

"Ma'am," the man said rather impatiently, "I can't tell

you how it works, just that it uses electricity. I even used it myself once."

Electricity! Everyone had seen the demonstrations on stage and in parlors of men bringing the sparkling element to life, even killing animals with it. There is no way I'll let that unpredictable demon into my house!

Etta thought about sending a note to David asking about it, but it might be hours before she got a reply. She hesitated.

"Ma'am, I have other orders to fill today. Are you going to let me in, or not?"

Her better judgment won out.

"I'm sorry, sir, but I must check with my husband first. You'll have to come back later." She loved how the term 'husband' sounded. As she walked back to the kitchen, she kept repeating, "my husband, my husband, MY HUSBAND."

Later that evening, when David arrived for supper, he inquired about the machine.

"Well, Darling, how do you like your new toy?" he asked with a smile. "You haven't called me on it yet."

Etta looked at Blanc, playing with a toy mouse in the corner. What the cleaning lady had missed, Blanc had found under the settee and bore little gray dust bunnies on her back.

"David, I didn't allow him in. You should have told me."

"Oh, then I'll have to re-schedule." With his usual meticulousness, he reached into his coat pocket and pulled out his gold pen and small notepad.

"Well, what is it? What kind of machine?" Etta said, feeling some chagrin at her conservativeness in refusing entry to the installer.

"Darling, you are due in two weeks. I need to know when your labor begins." David dove into another bite of gingerbread cake, pausing to chew it politely. "This machine allows you to talk to me directly, from this house to my office at the Palmer House."

"Talk directly? I don't understand. How can I do that?"

David summoned up more patience. Lord, women can be so irritating at times. "It's a box that sits on a table. Electricity sends your voice to me. When you call me, I can hear you and you can hear me."

Etta sat back with a jerk. How amazing! What was the world coming to, where your voice could travel over several blocks to someone in another place?

"Can I talk to Papa?" asked Etta.

"No, Love, just me. Maybe someday you can call other people, but as it works now, it's just me."

He went on, "This machine usually connects a man's home to his office, but I thought it could come in handy when your time comes." He cleared his throat. "There are fewer than 200 of these machines in the entire country." David puffed out his chest a bit with pride at his discovery of the new technological marvel.

The following day, Etta stood staring at the mahogany square box on her table. The hole in the center, about four inches across, was covered with a membrane. She tilted her head. How in the world can my voice travel through a box? She thought. What will they think of next—sending pictures?

David showed her how to use it. "Now, Love, you just lean towards this hole and yell my name very loud. If I don't answer, that means I am not at home or am indisposed."

"And you can hear me all the way in your hotel?"

Ah, women! thought David. They can be so obtuse! "Yes, you may have noticed a wire outside going from the house down the street. It travels all the way to my suite. Now watch, Darling, just do what I do." He yelled his name into the machine.

Etta listened. "There's no one there."

David's exasperation was growing by the minute. He had grand visions of machines like this transforming their lives and knew this was just the beginning.

"That's because I'm right here, Dear. I must be in my suite in order to answer you. Now, as soon as you call me, put your ear to the hole and listen for my voice. If there's no reply, yell into the machine and listen again. I may be out, so try again later."

"Can it hear everything I'm saying?" asked Etta. She didn't want David to know she talked to the cat.

Etta thought about all the times she had yelled at Blanc. Who will I end up calling if it hears me yell at Blanc? she wondered. Maybe I'd better start talking to her in French — just in case. Arrête ça!

"No, Dear, that's why you have to yell so loud. It only works if you yell into it."

After David left, Etta relaxed with Blanc sitting on her lap, staring at the machine. It had a mysterious power flowing through it that made it work. She wondered if it would harm the baby. He might think it's a great device, she thought, but I will use it only if I am forced to.

Years later, while having a later version of the telephone installed in his suite, David told his uncle about the machine debacle with Etta.

"Well," said Matthew with an amused smile, "It's a good thing women don't run the world." Uncle Matthew was crossing the room, pipe in hand, the other with his thumb hitched over his vest watch pocket. David smiled; he noticed the habit and thought about how that little gesture had once torn that very pocket, paving the way for him to visit Etta again.

Labor

Etta took up china painting again, a hobby she had a nodding acquaintance with from her single days in Pittsburgh. The Andrews Coat of Arms to be filled in on the porcelain face consisted of a red shield with green cross bars, topped by an armor faceplate, and yellow and red streaming ribbons on the sides.

Etta signed it on the back. At least now she had something to do to pass the days. Her depression lifted a bit. The tea Madam Vertina had sold her, drunk twice daily, lifted her spirits immensely.

David had finally accepted her flimsy excuse for being away the day Mrs. Parker came to clean. They eventually sorted out the incident between them, but Etta could not shake the feeling that the road just around the bend lay frightening, unknown obstacles. She would have to be more careful not to lose her beloved lover as her time neared. Her options had shrunk dramatically.

Finally, one day when she thought she couldn't stand one more minute of the long pregnancy, her labor began. June showered the month with new life all over the city.

Etta stood by the machine, hesitant to engage with it. What should I do? She thought about it between pains, took a deep breath and called David. To her surprise, he answered immediately and arrived shortly after with the midwife. She had a long labor, but David stayed by her side.

"It's a girl!" the midwife shouted.

Etta grimaced. She had so wanted to give David a son. An Andrews son. A son to become a member of the Andrews clan.

Living Together

David moved his little family to a larger apartment. Fortunately, most of the new neighbors assumed the couple was married.

Etta and David settled into a quasi-married routine with their new baby, named Claire after Etta's mother's middle name. David delighted playing with her, enjoying her sloppy kisses, hugs, baby talk, and first steps.

As remarkable a father as David proved to be during the first few months of his daughter's life, his attitude changed even more one day while feeding the baby in her high chair. He suddenly noticed familiar brown eyes looking directly at him. Great God, he thought, she is an Andrews. She must be my daughter! Once he fully understood that Etta may have conceived a child by him, he played with the baby more often and embraced her into his life.

Etta noticed the difference and wondered about the subtle change in David's treatment of Claire. She thought perhaps it was due to the infant wrapping around her lover's heart like vines latching onto an old stone wall. She didn't notice the family resemblance, having only seen fuzzy photos of his brothers in *The Tribune*.

Contentment evaded Etta in her new role. Her social life with David as a couple was limited. Why can't David and I go out — be a part of society? She wanted to be married. She wished he could forget her past association with the bordello and ride proudly with her and their baby in a carriage down State Street. She wanted to attend the balls, dine out, meet his family and friends, and be a party to his life outside the apartment. Now that Etta had lost her 'bump,' she could shop, go for walks, take her daughter to the park, and have lunch with friends in the new neighborhood. There could be more, oh yes, so much more to my life, she thought.

Then, an idea came to her one pleasant evening after supper; Etta, not looking up and pretending to tend to her knitting, quietly said, "David, have you ever thought about living someplace else?" She wanted a new start.

David didn't look up. The scene reminded Etta of that evening at the Palmer House when, over peas and potatoes, she told David she was expecting their child.

Her lover didn't ask "why." He knew why she posed this question.

The couple never spoke of Etta's work at the bordello. Everyone knew the reputations of the women who worked in them, no matter what their position was, even in a wild city like Chicago. The newly-rich in the mid-western city had to reach even farther back into their family heritages for blue blood, success, and sterling reputations. The gold and glitz added to nearly all the new Chicago buildings reflected Society's desire to run with the 'big boys' in New York and Paris.

David's family was no different. All the Andrews men

were in the *Social Register* and belonged to all the best clubs. The cloud of shame was not allowed to permeate their gilded mansions or private gatherings.

David smiled at her, reached over, and took her hand. Claire was prattling nearby in her high chair, playing with her mashed sweet potatoes.

"Dearest, you know I love Chicago. Our family came here from Virginia because my father, who is in real estate, saw enormous opportunity here after the fire. Chicago has been good to me and my family. Due to my father buying that property at Lake View, for all our Virginia friends, I have outstanding business and social connections here. I could never start over again in another city,"

Etta noted he didn't say "we." Her heart sank.

David took a bite of apple pie. "Delicious."

The Telegram

It seemed to Etta she had just cleaned up from Thanksgiving of 1880 when the Christmas holidays dashed upon her. Claire was eighteen months old, banging her spoon on the highchair and prattling. Etta, reading the paper and having coffee and a scone at the kitchen table, heard a knock at the door.

She opened the door. "Yes?" she asked, although the uniform answered before she finished the question. The boy leaned on his bicycle with one hand and handed Etta a telegram with the other.

"Thank you." She tipped the boy. Telegrams rarely bring good news if they come on a day not a holiday–too late for Thanksgiving and too early for Christmas greetings. She tore open the yellow envelope with a feeling of dread.

"HARRY IN ACCIDENT AT PLANT STOP BADLY BURNED STOP COME QUICKLY STOP"—from her stepmother Anne Ware in Pennsylvania.

Etta clutched the yellow paper to her chest—not her beloved papa! She jumped up, the suddenness of her movement bringing Claire to tears. She grabbed the child and rushed to her bedroom to assemble the many things needed when traveling with a toddler. A call to David went unanswered. Leaving him a note, she ran out into the cold and hailed a carriage to Union Station, not even checking the train schedule. Luckily, in just an hour, they were on their way.

Settling into their comfortable Pullman sleeping car, Etta couldn't help but recall the last time she rode the Pittsburgh-Chicago train line after meeting Billy Black. So much has happened—how little I knew back then. How happy—how mistaken—I was. No wonder I hate trains. None of them have taken me to a pleasant life, and now here I am, headed for what may be a funeral. She brushed the thoughts aside and began praying her papa would recover.

They arrived in Pittsburgh early the following morning and transferred to the branch train to Freeport. As a kindly stranger in his wagon drove her from the station to her papa's house, Etta noted no snow had visited that part of Pennsylvania.

Anne opened the door, face swollen and tear-streaked. "Etta," she cried and fell into her arms. "I am so sorry. I sent the last wire as soon as I could."

Etta stared at her. "What?" She exclaimed, sensing the bad news.

"He didn't make it through the night."

Later, Anne spoke of the horrific accident while sitting in the warm parlor. "Harry had just arrived at work at the distillery. It was about five in the morning."

She paused, collecting herself. "He went into the room containing the copper still while holding a lantern. They have no idea exactly what happened, but the still exploded. They think it was his lantern that started the fire. Harry was burned over most of his body. He suffered for a whole hour before the fireman could find him." She stopped, sobbing, "They could hear his screams, but the smoke was so thick and the fire so hot they couldn't get near him. The entire distillery burned to the ground. And the morning newspapers are blaming him for the explosion."

Etta sat, horrified at the agony her beloved papa must have felt. She began to sob. She had wanted to arrive in time to tell him goodbye—to be there for him the way he always was for her. Now he was gone. "Oh, God!" sobbed Etta. "Oh, My God!" She thought about all the battles he had survived during the Civil War. How ironic—he was simply going to work that fateful dark morning.

"But, at least, death relieved him of the pain," Anne went on. "He was in agony, begging someone to shoot him." She broke into sobs again.

Silence enveloped the two women. Claire played outside with her cousins. Their laughter and screams of joy pierced the grief of the stepmother and daughter like crystal shattering on a marble floor.

The Funeral

All Etta's half-siblings and their children attended the funeral. Of course, everyone wondered about Claire. Etta had thought a good deal on the train about how she would explain the little girl's existence. *She is nearly two, so how can I explain the years when everyone believed me to be a widow?* She had muddled about the problem from Indiana through Ohio.

Maybe I should tell them I adopted her? Or I found her on the street one dismal rainy day? As the miles flew by, the more absurd her ideas became. She realized she had to develop a story the entire family would believe. She decided the safest tale to tell was that she had been raped, a partial truth. *That will make me a victim rather than a whore.*

Etta's stepmother Anne inquired first. "And the little girl?" Anne nodded toward Claire, happily playing with dolls on the floor.

"Chicago can be a dangerous city," Etta began. "And I was so naive. One late night someone burst into my house, grabbed me, and threw me on the floor. He then proceeded to violate me."

Anne shook her head in dismay as Claire chided her dollies for spilling their tea.

"After the attack, I was in the hospital with bruises and broken ribs but was able to return home a few days later." Etta cleared her throat and paused.

"I made a decision. And the result was my little love over there." She nodded toward her daughter.

"Oh, Etta, I am so sorry," replied her stepmother, touching her shoulder gently.

"Don't be—thank you anyway," replied Etta. "She is a true joy."

Except for one sibling whispering, "What a shame it is– the little girl will never know who her father is," no one questioned Claire's existence again.

Back in Chicago, Etta opened the second telegram. Her half-empty coffee cup and scone were still on the kitchen table. A marching trail of ants led from the window sill to the scone. "Father died 4:30 a .m.," it read.

The Muff

Two years later, in 1882, significant changes were sweeping across the country with the birth of Standard Oil, the first Labor Day, the invention of the clothes iron, and the first electrical power plant built in New York. The Temperance Union's efforts failed to dam the steady flow of liquor in Chicago and the accompanying crime, abuse, and deaths.

Claire was growing and developing as well. Her engaging with people and her developing personality endeared her to those around her. Born with a ferocious temper and dominant personality, Claire kept her mother busy. As much as Etta adored children, the little girl proved to be a handful.

Before Etta knew it, Claire had celebrated her fourth birthday. A bit stockier than other girls her age, her strong will had begun to show its force.

Claire wanted a muff. She had seen children and grown women, hands at their waists, glorious black, white, and even brown luxury furs lined with satin, hugging and warming cold hands. The little girl thought they were the most beautiful things she had ever seen.

She began harassing Etta and David for one. "Mother, I need a MUFF." Not "I WANT a muff," but, "I NEED a muff."

Because of the exorbitant expense of a gift like that for a child so young, Etta wanted to discuss the matter with David. She believed he spoiled his daughter and attributed his doing so to his feeling he had to compensate the apparent deficit in her life—that of her not having a 'real' father.

"Mother?" Claire repeated, punching Etta's knee to get her attention and rousing her mother out of her reverie. "Can't you get one for me?"

"I'll talk to David about it," Etta replied.

Etta privately pleaded with him not to take on the expenditure. Her beloved mate could often be seen vacillating regarding the discipline of the tiny terror. Etta held her breath as she watched the scene play out. David paced the oriental carpet, rubbing his chin and stuttering a bit. But when the order came, it marched out like a determined soldier.

"Claire, no muff, Darling, not yet." I am so proud of him, Etta thought, with a tiny smile.

Claire threw herself on the floor, screaming and kicking. "I want a MUFF! I want a MUFF!"

"Claire," said David over the shouting, "I'm telling you what you are doing will not get you any closer to having one. Now stop that immediately."

Etta watched her daughter, shaking her head. That temper would not parse well for her throughout the child's life. She silently wondered how she could cure her of the outbursts. She hoped the little girl had not learned it from her–she had tried so hard to hide her tantrums from her daughter, even sometimes managing to use restraint long enough to get Claire out of the room when she felt her own rage coming on. She thought she had gained some control as she learned to recognize the tightness in her chest just before the explosions erupted, which helped a bit.

Etta plucked up the child and put her to bed, sobbing.

A year later, Claire got her gift, a beautiful white fur muff.

"How do you like your new muff?" David asked her with a broad smile.

"I hate it, it makes my hands sweaty. And I can't run or do anything outside with it, like playing. The only time I like it is when it's cold out and I'm riding in the carriage."

Within a week, Claire dropped the muff from the carriage and watched it blend with the white snow until a trolley wheel ground it into the street, swallowed by the gray slush.

Claire never looked back.

Where's My Daddy?

The inevitable occurred. Etta knew it would arise one day, like a blade of crabgrass showing up unexpectedly. She had spent months, her mind chewing on the problem like a dog with a worn bone, trying to decide how to answer her daughter.

"Mommy, where's my daddy? Why can't I call David 'daddy'?"

Claire, now six, had enough young friends in the neighborhood to be aware of 'normal' families. Her friends noticed that she didn't call David 'daddy' and asked her about it. Claire always flushed with embarrassment. She wanted to fit in, not stand out. She still went by the surname 'King'.

Etta didn't reply right away. She had to be so careful what she said. These words would fly, return, dip, and soar for the rest of the girl's life. They had to be perfect. Claire would run up against the 'truth' the rest of the family had held for all of Etta's life—that she had married Charles King, who died in an accident in 1876 in Chicago–that she had no man in her life when Claire was born two years later.

"Your daddy is in Heaven," Etta explained, caressing her daughter's dark hair. The big brown eyes looked up at her.

"Can he come back?" Claire asked. "Can he come on the trolley?"

Her innocence pained Etta to watch. "No, people don't come back from Heaven, dearest." Before she could continue, Claire burst into tears and threw her notebook, shattering a lamp.

"I want my daddy. I want my daddy to come back. NOW! RIGHT NOW." She screamed like a drunken banshee through her sobs.

"Shhhh," Etta murmured. "It's all right, baby, you have me, and David, and". . . poor child, she doesn't have anyone else, she thought.

Claire finally fell asleep in her mother's lap. Etta felt horrid. She dreaded future questions from her daughter, which she knew would increase as the child got older and became more aware. She thought back to the day she decided to get pregnant. Oh, dear God, she thought. What have I done?

Lunch at the Union League Club

David scheduled a luncheon with one of his clients one Wednesday morning. Howard, the doorman, pulled open the heavy doors of the Union League Club, where David had been a member for several years. David handed his coat and hat to the coat checker. "How have you been, Lucy?" he asked her.

The girl, young and attractive, smiled at David. "Just fine, Mr. Andrews, and you?"

"Oh, things are going quite well," David replied. "How is your search for a new apartment going? Have you found anything yet?"

"Well, I'm still looking," Lucy responded. "I may have found something over on Halstead Street, but I am still not sure I can afford it. I'm looking for another girl to help share the expenses."

"Well, good luck, then, and if I run across something, I'll let you know."

"Thank you, Mr. Andrews. I'd appreciate that."

David strode up the stairs up to the second-floor library. He had a little time before his lunch appointment and wanted to read. He strolled to the Classics section and ran his finger along the shelf until he found the play, *The Taming of the Shrew*, one of his favorites.

He ran his hand over the worn leather cover. He loved memorizing quotes from Shakespeare for apropos injections into conversations. He chose a chair by the window and began reading.

"Is she so hot a shrew as reported?"

"She was, good Curtis, before this frost. But thou knows't winter man, woman, and beast, for it hath tamed my old master and my new mistress. . ."

Later, David greeted his client with a hearty handshake and pointed to a table in the corner. Most Union League Club members liked to be seen, but David preferred the privacy of a table in the corner.

The young man across from David also earned his living as a land investor. Though he had a few rough edges, they did not prevent him from prospering. However, when he had entered the dining room, he carried his overcoat over his arm, which brought an instant admonition from the maitre d'.

"No overcoats allowed in the dining room, Sir," he said, with an upturned nose preceded by a sniff.

The young guest, embarrassed, tried to take control of the situation by replying, "Oh, sorry, would you mind taking it downstairs for me?"

Shocked, the maitre d' signaled to a waiter to do the favor.

After exchanging niceties and ordering, David and his guest got down to business.

After a lunch of vichyssoise, lobster roll, and fresh

spring peas, the man casually said, "When are you going to marry that woman, David? I hear you have a daughter by her."

David bristled. He had heard the gossip about him and his former Martha Webster employee. He tried his best to quell rumors about their relationship but knew that if he acted defensively, it would make him look guilty.

"I have no idea what you are talking about, Gregory," David replied. "Now, how about coffee?"

Columbian Exposition

The first hot day of the summer of June 1890 found the little Andrews family enjoying a day at the beach. Everyone was dressed according to the fashion of the day, covered head to toe in dark wool fabrics and even hats and gloves. From a distance, the scene looked as though the shore was swarming with lazy black ants–some strolling, some sitting, some venturing a toe in the cold water of Lake Michigan. A light breeze from the east increased the pleasure of the crowd.

David's family sat on the beach, David enjoying a cigar, as Claire drew pictures in the white sand. Etta gazed out at the blue water.

"Well, it looks as though we're going to get the Fair." said David to no one in particular.

"What fair?" asked Claire, envisioning food and rides.

"The Columbian Exposition," replied David with a smile. "It's going to be the biggest thing that has happened to this city since the Great Fire."

"What is a Columbian Exposition?" asked Claire, stumbling over the words, a quizzical look on her face. It sounded too complicated to be much fun.

"The 400th anniversary of the discovery of America by Christopher Columbus," interrupted Etta. "Chicago won the bid over Philadelphia, New York, and St. Louis, and it's going to last the whole summer. Frederick Olmstead, the designer of Central Park in New York, is going to head up the team."

"Yes," David continued for her. "Olmstead got a wonderful group of designers together, and we are all hoping this event will finally put our great city on the map. Countries worldwide will be represented, and you will get to see all of the latest inventions."

"Sounds so boring," complained Claire. She had her fill of studying foreign countries in the history class at the exclusive private girls' school she attended.

"Well," said Etta, ever tuned in to her daughter's more tactile leanings. "There will be dozens of exotic restaurants, and best yet, loads of fun rides. And everything is going to be painted white; it's going to be so beautiful."

Clair's ears perked up—she jumped up, destroying her sand picture of a dog with a bone. "Really? Oh!" She clapped her hands. "I can't wait! When is it coming?"

"It isn't coming," said David. "It has to be built, down at Jackson Park. It's going to take a long time to finish, but it will bring lots of young men in from all over the country to help construct it." he added.

Claire pouted. She hated waiting for anything. "I'm going to be an old maid by the time they get it done." She sat down with a plop and started a new drawing with her stick in the sand.

Coming of Age

The closing decade of the nineteenth century flew by. To Etta, the years seemed like months; the months like weeks. Claire was growing like the city, upward, relentless, and complex.

One sparkling day, arms crossed, thumbs wriggling, Etta paced back and forth, the light from the tall windows of her house catching and releasing her body into the shadows. She said, "we have to do something about her. She is out of control."

David, snug in his cashmere sweater and easy chair, nodded slowly. Uncle Matthew sat by a window so he could feel the warmth from the sun, one leg crossed over the other, open newspaper about to fall off his generous lap.

"We've tried everything—ballet, needlework, scrapbooking..." She paused and looked at her husband. "Nothing sticks. She's either too clumsy or bored."

"How about photography?" Uncle Matthew ventured.

Etta stopped, hands still folded. "Photography? You mean taking people's portraits?"

"No, they have cameras for us ordinary folk now. You

don't need a studio. You can simply go out and find something interesting, point the camera at it, and press a button. Then you have your own picture."

Etta glanced at David. He had looked up with interest and was nodding.

"A company called Kodak makes them," added Matthew.

"Cost?" queried David, remembering the funds he had poured into other frivolous pursuits of his daughter.

Uncle cocked his head and twisted his mouth a bit. "Oh, let's see—I looked at one last week. It's about six dollars now, considerably less since its introduction a couple of years ago."

"That sounds reasonable," said Etta as she took a chair by David. "What do you think, darling?"

David looked over at his uncle. "Any other costs?"

"Well, of course, you have to get the film processed. Each roll holds 100 pictures." He paused. "You will have to mail the camera back to the manufacturer to get it done."

The three sat quietly, processing the information. Perhaps a hobby like that would give their daughter purpose, maybe even calm her down.

"Doesn't she have a birthday coming up?" Matthew asked. A robin was trilling right outside the window. He tapped his cigar. "I'll get her one."

Claire sat at the head of the table, laden with gifts. A birthday cake from the William Schmidt Bakery sat before her, its thirteen candle flames waving happily in the afternoon light. As she opened her presents, she displayed little emotion, but when she pulled the wrapping paper off the Kodak, she shouted, "A camera! I've heard about them. My friend Becky has one!" Forgetting about her cake and guests, she pushed back her chair, causing the aging Blanc to leap out of her way. And out she ran, to the sidewalk in front of the house. As she looked up and down the street, a ragged dog came limping along the street. Claire raised her camera. The dog approached. Click, wind. The dog looked up at her with a haggard stare. Click, wind. The dog turned and quickly stepped back as a noisy carriage approached. Click, wind.

Etta appeared at the door. "Claire! What are you doing! You have guests!"

"Just a second, Mother." Click, at the retreating cur.

"Claire! Get back in here! You're being rude!"

Claire reluctantly took one last shot as the dog painfully made his way down the street. "Yes, Mother."

Uncle Matthew's choice of the new hobby for his niece was successful. Claire loved playing with her new toy, taking pictures of anything that commanded her interest: windswept corners, ladies' hats, sunsets in multi-shades of grey, boat crashes on the Chicago River—even interesting doorways she passed. It took her a while to remember to wind the film to the next frame, so she ended up with quite a few interesting double exposure prints.

She also adored school and especially her life as a city girl. Besides taking pictures, her favorite pastime was going out to lunch.

Etta and Claire entered Tivoli Gardens around noon; the pair's moods reflected the brilliance of the late summer day in September.

After being seated, the two examined the menu.

"Try the oyster stew," instructed Etta. "It's the best in town."

Claire, who had just turned thirteen, turned up her

nose. "No, mother, I don't think so." She turned her attention back to the menu and ordered a cheese sandwich.

"Oh, my goodness gracious, Claire. You are truly not ordering a cheese sandwich in one of the finest restaurants in Chicago!"

Claire bowed her head. Shame had become a familiar companion to her, frequently conveyed in acidic tones from her mother.

After a lovely dessert of blanc mange, they arose from the table. As Claire turned to leave, Etta grabbed her daughter's arm. "Claire! What is that on your dress?"

Claire stopped. Her mother seemed unusually alarmed. Have I spilled something? Claire wondered.

Etta bent down and looked at the back of Claire's dress. A small red stain announced where she had been sitting.

Agitated, her mother shouted, "Claire! No!"

"What, Mother?" Claire said in a pleading tone. She had learned over the years not to cross her mother. Goodness knows what I have done this time. Undoubtedly, the infraction hadn't been using the wrong utensil, as they had finished lunch.

Etta, following close behind, pushed Claire to the washroom. There, she used a towel and water to diminish the spot announcing to the world that her daughter had reached womanhood.

Whatever she had done, Claire had made her mother furious.

Now we would have to go home in the public cars– where everyone could see.

When they arrived home, Etta had Claire remove her dress and underclothes and gave her cotton batten and pins. "Put this on so you don't soil the furniture!" Etta demanded.

Claire had no idea what had happened. I'm bleeding! Why doesn't Mother call the doctor? Why is she so angry? But better not ask. Etta never said anything about the facts of life to her daughter. Claire later learned about them from her friends at school. How could every woman go through this and I never even heard of it, she wondered, struggling with the pins and batten. What kind of a world is this, anyway?

Claire pouted around her mother for the rest of the week.

Hawking Biscuits

The Fair lasted from April until the end of October, with the entrance fee costing twenty-five cents. Everyone wanted to see and be seen. Etta did not wish to be an exception and donned her finest white lace dress and bonnet. Claire wore a peach design with ribbons, lace, and flower inserts.

Overwhelmed by the number of exhibitions, the pair had made a list of 'must-sees' beforehand. First on Etta's list was the painted mural in the Women's Hall by the American artist Mary Cassatt, depicting the dawning of the Women's Movement and burgeoning women's independence. Women were intrigued with the possibility of not having to observe the familiar New Year's Eve tradition of kneeling before their husbands and apologizing for being such 'bad wives'.

Claire grabbed her mother's hand. "Oh, Mother. We must visit the Chicago Wheel! My friends told me it is truly amazing. It takes you 'way up in the sky, around and around. You can see all over the city!"

George Ferris' invention debuted at the Fair. The pods

held up to sixty people each, and nine minutes was all it took for the wheel to make one revolution. Riders raved about the experience for years afterward.

The pair headed toward the exhibit when Etta suddenly stopped. "Wait!" She told Claire. "Shhh. Be quiet!"

"What?"

"Claire, HUSH! I'm trying to hear something." Etta had heard a familiar voice saying the Andrews name.

Claire looked at her mother, curious about what would draw her attention in this crowd.

"Come!" She pushed Claire and headed toward the voice.

There, on a stage, stood the Andrews family cook, Sallie Reed, bright apron covering her ample stomach, making biscuits. A huge billboard nearby advertised the flour company with a painting of her and a banner that read, 'Cousin Sallie's Biscuits.'

Sallie stood at a large table with a wooden spoon, a giant bowl of dough, a white apron, and a chef's hat. Stirring and smiling, she said, "An' that 'lil Jimmy, he come a' runnin' wi' that bear right on his tail."

The crowd cheered and clapped. All day Sallie handed out her delicious biscuits and told stories of the Andrews family boys back in old Virginia.

She never seemed to spot Etta in the crowd.

"Mother. Why are we stopping here? I want to go on the Chicago Wheel!" whined Claire. She rarely saw her mother make biscuits. Etta rarely got out of bed 'til after lunch.

"Oh, she just reminded me of someone I used to know," said Etta.

"Who, that person up there on the stage?" said Claire. "From where? I never knew you had HELP."

"Well, it was a long time ago, Dear–it's no one who would interest you."

They moved on to the next exhibit, when Claire noticed her mother's mood had changed. She knew not to ask any more questions.

A Second Visit

Etta returned to the fair alone the next day. Etta listened to the warm voice of Sallie Reed–'Cousin Sallie'–rolling over the rapt crowd.

"And, Mastah Petie, he come a'running toward the house, screaming and yellin' like you ain't never heard, a whole bunch of bees right on his tail. I was fetching water, and just threw that whole bucket on him, grabbed his hand, and we both set out running for the outhouse. We ran in there, slammed the door shut, and just set down laughing, that Petie and me." The spectators roared with laughter.

The crowd grew so large the biscuit company had to hire guards to keep it moving, but Etta kept returning. Sallie told more stories of life in Virginia, living with two of the Walker boys. Etta stayed until the stories began to repeat themselves.

Sallie never once mentioned David. It was as though he had never existed in her life. She prayed David would never hear of this. It would only exacerbate his feelings of isolation.

The Fire

July 5, 1893—Etta dabbed away with a brush at her new china plate. She stopped to look out the window at the steamy day. Heat radiated up from the macadam street and sucked the moisture from the leaves of the trees. Birds had taken the day off, hiding in shady nooks in the city. David would not be home for supper and Claire was staying overnight with a friend.

Later that evening, after putting her painting supplies away and finishing a small meal, she heard the clatter of hooves and fire bells outside clanging like wild apparitions banging on pots with wooden spoons. The abandoned Fairgrounds were afire. The blaze began in the Woman's Building and quickly spread to the other structures. The fire chief believed vagabonds squatting in the empty structure started the blaze. Workers who had rushed to Chicago to work at constructing the Exposition were, two years later, now jobless, penniless and living in the empty buildings. The night sky and the lake shimmered with gold as half of Chicago stood on the streets, balconies, and at windows, watching the fire.

She leaned her head back against the chair. The brilliant orange sky took her back to a night over a decade ago, on another hot July day in another city. The fireworks of that night in the little town near Pittsburgh flared in her memory. It seems so long ago. She closed her eyes and mentally returned to the day she met Billy Black. How handsome he was. She remembered their first kiss, the smell of him—how his clothes had absorbed the odors of Pittsburgh after just a few days in the steel city. She had grown to love that smell in the few weeks they were together—a mixture of soot, steel, and cheap cologne.

It felt like true love at the time, she thought to herself. But it was child's play compared to my feelings for David.

How different my life would have turned out if I had married Billy as I believed. He probably would have been hired as a construction worker for the Fair. Now there would be no money, a houseful of children, and the constant sour shame that always accompanies poverty.

She imagined passing David on LaSalle Street before they had met. Would she have noticed him? His fine clothes, elegant demeanor, and the whiff of expensive cologne would have attracted her attention. Would they have stopped, talked–despite that type of familiarity being forbidden by society–even had an affair? She dozed off and dreamt of billowing smoke and glowing ashes.

The Healthy Man

David dropped his towel as he stepped out of the bath and into his bedroom at the Palmer House.

He stood naked in front of the tall mirror mounted on its ornate carved swivelled stand. He stared at the reflection of his body in the early morning light.

Not bad for an old man, he thought to himself, even though he was turning only forty. He drew in his breath and puffed out his chest, holding the pose for a moment. He then flexed his arm and shoulder muscles, bending over and to the side. He turned and tried to see his back, but could see only fat cheeks and hairy legs.

The entire country was caught up in a movement to improve the physiques of American men. Brought on by the writings of Bernarr McFadden, papers and magazines were touting advice for American males on how to garner strength, improve health and live longer lives. Up to that point, most men thought little about the physicality under their clothing.

David was no exception. Although he led an active life through his profession, which involved quite a bit of walking, he rarely thought of bodily improvements. But now, determined not to be left behind by this latest craze, he took the time to examine himself.

He turned and looked down at his manly parts. He admitted he was a bit envious of his father and uncle's more generous endowments. "But it's what I do with it that counts," he whispered to himself. Although sex between them was, at this point, practically routine, he still felt the need to hold Etta's interest.

Etta had not been David's first sexual encounter. He found a relationship while in college with a randy redhead, and, through several encounters, learned enough about sex to begin to be able to control himself. By the time he got to Etta, he was rather sophisticated regarding satisfying a woman.

A Warning

David picked up the phone on his desk at his office.

"David?" He recognized his uncle Matthew's voice immediately. "Meet me at my club for lunch. We need to talk."

David wondered what Matthew wanted to discuss. Even though they were close, they had little time to spend with one another since Matthew had married. I hope it's about a new real estate deal, David thought.

The two took their seats in the maroon and mahogany dining room of the elegant Chicago Club and exchanged information about the exploding real estate market as cultured low voices hummed around them.

"David, I've been hearing rather unpleasant rumors about you."

David knew immediately where this talk was going. Uncle Matthew was aware of his involvement with the former employee of Martha Webster, but that was the extent of his knowledge.

"Yes, she has a child. I'm supporting them." David didn't look up.

"Son..."

Uncle Matthew went on about the family's reputation, being responsible, and so on. David, mindlessely moving the peas on his plate around, had heard all this before and heaved a heavy sigh.

"There's talk of your being dropped from the *Social Register*. You need to either separate yourself, or marry the girl. The Andrews' family's honor is at stake. People are beginning to gossip. And you know it won't bode well for you if your father finds out about your living situation."

David knew all too well that his uncle was right — Chicago Society was a small city with a big mouth.

David sat in a barber chair at the Palmer House. "The usual, George," he instructed the barber. His mind wandered to the conversation with his uncle the week before. Tearing myself from my lover and daughter would be like tearing off my own skin. I can't do it. He sighed and sank farther back in the leather chair, the razor's swish-swish calming his thoughts.

A few weeks later, responding to a call from his father, David sat across from James in the library of his Lake View mansion, not in a restaurant or club. James wanted to avoid long ears picking up the conversation.

He's getting a bit of a paunch, David thought, noticing his father's spreading middle. James had just celebrated his sixty-fifth birthday. I hope I don't get that way when I am his age.

His father clasped his hands and cleared his throat. The pair had seen little of one another since their trip to Denver. David tried to avoid any of the family's inquiring eyes or raised brows by replying with 'previous commitments' regarding the few invitations he received for family functions. He didn't like the feelings of isolation that always accompanied him on those visits, no matter how crowded the room with his family.

James poured each a shot of bourbon and sat down across from his son. He spoke, "David, I think you know why I asked you here today."

His father seemed even more distant than usual.

David nodded, braced for the fall of the hammer.

"Your sister Abigail has met someone. Someone significant. As you may know, she's on the list for British Royals of eligible American heiresses."

High society members all over the country were aware of the crush of single British royals to the United States in search of wealthy young women to marry and become rescue vehicles for their dwindling family fortunes.

"And that has created some promising introductions for her. One suitor seems to be rather serious. But there is a problem." He stopped and looked over at his son.

David nodded. He could have written the script word-for-word before this meeting.

"The Earl is telling us he cannot enter into a marriage to someone with scandal attached to her family name." He stopped to brush an imaginary piece of lint off his lapel and took a sip of bourbon.

"I believe Matthew talked to you, but he tells me there has been no change in your present living situation." He paused. "I'm afraid I am being forced to disown you."

There–there it was–clear as crystal–the choice between his Andrews family or his love. The final rejection by the illustrious Virginia family.

The statement rang in David's ear. It seemed to take on a life of its own, like a vulture hovering over a smelly carcass. James went on about how he hoped David would understand the importance of this marriage to the family, to its name and reputation, its elevation—to sit amongst the highest of the high–marriage of an old Virginia family into British Royalty.

David felt as though he had foreseen this conversation–like watching a speeding carriage out of control, headed straight for him–and that there was nothing he could do. He stood, nodded to his father, and left the room. As the front door slammed shut, his half-drunk amber bourbon shimmered in its crystal glass. There was nothing more to be said. The familial scissors had cut the cord.

In the Paper

Etta sipped the last of her coffee. The steam rolled into her sinuses, freeing them from the night's congestion. She loved breakfast the most of any meal of the day, even though the clock had just struck noon —another new day–hours of opportunity, another chance to make the most of her life.

Claire had left for school and David for work. Alone in the house, Etta arose from the kitchen chair to collect the paper. She turned to the Society section of *The Tribune*. On page 30, there it was–

> "One of the most notable of the functions of the week was the marriage on Wednesday (June 5) of Miss Abigail Andrews, a daughter of the late James Andrews, and of Mrs. James J. Andrews, to (*.*), son of Hon. (*.*), Earl of (*.*), England, whose home is at (*.*) England. In attendance were the Messrs. David P. Andrews, . . ."

She reread it and slammed the paper down onto her lap. David Andrews? At the wedding? She rose, enraged. He had lied to her. He said he would see about our attending that wedding, and now I have to read that he went without me about it in the paper! David had never shared the latest information regarding his status with his father and the Andrews family with her.

Furious, she stared out the front window onto the busy street below. "Just you wait 'til you get home," she yelled aloud. An alarmed sparrow darted off the window sill.

An hour later, the ticking hand on the clock found Etta sobbing on her bed and thinking–what good is it to be living with one of Chicago's elite if you are kept in the closet like a family skeleton? Her moods switched between rage and tears. She would let him know. She would never let him forget this slight. She would leave him and go back to Pennsylvania. She would stop speaking to him. She would turn him out of her bed. Resolute, she arose and began packing her trunk. She would be gone when he got home. She would leave him a note. No, she would not leave a note. Let him comb the streets looking for me, twisting and turning at night as his imagination drove sleep from him.

So, who would you be punishing, Etta, him or you? A little voice inside her whispered.

The Explanation

David's footsteps echoed down the hall—he opened the door to the parlor and stepped inside. He ducked, unable to see what was headed his way, as Etta threw the newspaper at him.

Standing upright, he stared at her standing by the window. She looked furious.

What is it this time? he wondered.

"Just look at that." Etta screamed.

David calmly took off his hat and hung it on the rack. He bent down and picked up the paper, wondering what provoked this tantrum. He looked at her, smoothed out the page, and began to read aloud, "David P. Andrews..."

He looked up, waiting for a response, but she said nothing. David reread it louder. "David **P.** Andrews."

Etta's face dropped. Her entire body slumped as she realized what she had done. David P. Andrews was a distant cousin. She had misread the name and jumped to an erroneous conclusion. She felt so stupid and embarrassed she didn't know what to say.

David was accustomed to living with people with

tempers. His father's rages after his wife's death would have terrified him as a young boy had he not had Sallie Reed's full skirts to find refuge behind. He had learned to mentally remove himself from such dramatic scenes.

David walked over to her and put his arms around her. "Everyone makes mistakes, Love." He took a deep breath. "Even you."

After History Class

Claire stopped to tie her shoe. "Wait." she called to her friends, newly released from the boredom of her private school's history class and greeting the freedom of the afternoon. Spring had drawn out the colorful tree blossoms. Happy at her school but not particularly popular, Claire had nonetheless acquired one close friend, Becky.

The little group plopped down on the expansive lawn, greener due to the spring and sending up the smell of freshly mown grass.

"What shall we do?" said Becky.

"Let's get something to eat!" shouted Millie, whose size already advertised her love of food.

"I'm not hungry," Jill responded.

The group fell silent, soaking in the promise of the day and the sounds of the breeze humming to its beauty.

The cold gray stones of the old building stood in sharp contrast to the youth, the energy, and the joy of the little group of girls.

"You know what we heard yesterday?" said Caroline, a tiny blonde.

"What?" The girls shouted in unison.

"Tell them, Maude!" said Caroline with a wicked grin.

Maude, a lanky sandy-haired beauty, leaned down and whispered her juicy gossip tidbit. The group exploded in laughter, some pounding the ground.

"I can believe it!" laughed Jill, with her freckles and sandy hair. "She always looked as though she had a big secret!"

The laughter subsided as the girls reflected on what each would have done had she been in that position.

Claire had to go to the bathroom. "I'll be right back." she shouted as she ran back toward the granite building. "Don't talk about me," she shot back with a giggle.

Maude watched her walk away. "Do you know what I heard about her mother?" she gestured toward Claire, now with the walking the 'wriggle walk' as she had to go so badly. The girls leaned in.

When she returned, Claire noticed a chill had enveloped the group. They were playing with the grass, looking for four-leafed clovers. No one spoke. She pulled a long blade, held it to her nose, then began trying to fold it into a knot.

Finally, she raised her head. "So, what did I miss?" she asked.

No one spoke, and the little group looked nervously at one another. "What's wrong?" Claire asked, feeling a little lump rising in her throat. Becky leaned over and patted her hand. "It's all right," she whispered.

The Bully

Claire stood in the cafeteria line, choosing a slice of ham, a generous helping of macaroni and cheese and a salad. The buxom, red-headed girl behind her leaned closer, her mouth inches from Claire's ear.

"I know what your mother did," she whispered, then quickly pulled away, still holding Claires gaze, a sneer on her face. Claire turned and stared at her.

"What," she gulped. She didn't like this girl, who had a reputation for being a gossip and a bully.

The girl leaned back, giggled, looked around to see if anyone else was listening, said, "Your mother worked in the Levee District."

Claire understood there was little worse anyone could have said about a woman. Everyone knew the reputation of the tawdry neighborhood.

Claire stared at the girl. I must be hearing things. She didn't know what to do or say. In shock, she held her tray and looked around the room. Who had heard? Who else knew? She wanted to die.

The Cards

The room seemed dark, save a small shaft of morning light falling across the paisley table covering. Madam Vertina once again sat across from Etta.

"What is it, my dear," she asked. The two had not communicated for quite some time.

Etta had rung the seer early that morning, and the old woman had been able to clear her calendar for an hour.

"Claire is in the hospital. She tried to take her life," she sobbed.

Madam sat quietly. A fly buzzed around a crumb on the floor.

"You know what happened?" asked Madam.

"No, I don't," wailed Etta. "The school called this morning and said they couldn't wake her. They had already called an ambulance. She is at Baptist Hospital. They don't know if she is going to live." Etta lowered her head as the sobs seized her body. "They found an empty container of pills by her bed. They don't know where she got them or what they were."

Madam let Etta continue.

"What could have made her do this?" Etta looked at her seer imploringly.

"You should be there," Madam murmured with a scowl. Etta's visit to her instead of the hospital told Madam more about Etta than anything the mother said.

"I'm going, from here. Please tell me, is my daughter going to live?"

"We ask cards." The gypsy placed a deck of Tarot cards on the table. "You know these?"

Etta shook her head. She had used an Ouija board before, but never these. Larger than playing cards, they displayed colorful images of people in various states of what looked like acrobats. Madam Vertina fanned out the cards and selected one. Her deep gentle voice calmed Etta.

The first card was that of the Magician. Madam smiled. "She going to be fine," she said with a smile. The next, the Wheel of Fortune, reversed. "You both be changing. New life." She laid down the Strength card next. And lastly, the Chariot.

"Everything going to be fine. You see, my dear?" smiled Madam. "Cards never lie." She held out her other hand for the payment.

The reading reassured Etta by her repeating the meanings of the cards to herself as she made her way to the hospital. "She's going to be all right," she kept repeating. "She's going to be fine."

The Decision

The school expressed reluctance at allowing Claire to return.

"Perhaps a year off," the headmistress suggested with a false smile. David and Etta agreed.

Several months later, David learned from his physician brother Peter what had driven his daughter to such a drastic act. He knew the cruel girl's family but decided not to stir the pot by confronting her parents. Claire would never be returning to that school. But the crisis led David down a path he had never traversed before. He made his decision, threw on his coat and hat, hailed a carriage, and headed for the ornate art deco doors of C. D. Peacock's, Jewelers.

Claire Awakes

Claire slowly opened her eyes. Everything was blurry, and she didn't know where she was. Where was Mother—David?

She raised herself on one elbow and looked around at the all-white room. She saw no rug, curtains, or anything that felt like a home. On a small table sat a pitcher of water and a glass. Her iron bed occupied a corner, and nearby stood a small chair. A stab of fear coursed through her body. She started to shake. Am I in a nightmare? Her throat was sore, as though she had been vomiting.

A strange woman, all dressed in white with a starched cap, entered the room.

"Well, Miss Claire, how are we feeling?"

Claire was confused. Who was this 'we'? She didn't reply.

The woman continued. "You gave us all quite a scare, young lady," she smiled, shaking a glass rod in her hand and approaching Claire.

Claire shrank back. What was that? Where was that lady going to put it?

"Open up." The woman demanded.

Clair lay back, trying to melt into the bed.

"Dear, we have to take your temperature. It doesn't hurt. You just hold it under your tongue for one minute, and don't talk, all right?"

Well, maybe that won't be so bad. But it tasted horrid, and Claire wanted to spit it out. But she did as told, not once taking her huge brown eyes off this strange lady.

"That's a good girl. Now, please give me your wrist. I have to check your pulse."

Claire knew how a pulse was taken from science class, so she complied. She was still wary but couldn't bring herself to ask where she was. She didn't want to look stupid or as if she had amnesia or something. Maybe I can figure it out after the lady is gone.

The nurse turned to leave. "They'll be bringing you something to eat in a few minutes. You'll feel much better."

That proved to be true. She did feel better but still felt confused and frightened. After supper, she lay stiff as a board, afraid to move or ask anyone what had happened or where she was.

"Hello, Darling!" Etta swept into the room, pheasant hat feathers bobbing a cheery 'hello'. Her mother's voice sounded forced, artificial. Claire didn't answer; instead, she burst into tears, grabbing her mother, hugging her tight.

"I don't know what happened." she sobbed. "Where am I? Why am I here?"

Etta looked stunned. Her daughter didn't remember anything? How could she tell her? What should she tell her?

Claire continued sobbing while Etta tried to think of what to say.

"You had an accident, Darling, and are in the hospital."

"What happened? Where? When?"

"Don't tire yourself, Dearest, we'll talk about it later. Now you just rest. I'll come to visit every day."

Every day? What is wrong with me? Despite feeling extremely groggy, Claire didn't hurt anywhere. She hadn't broken any bones; she felt sure of that, as she saw no casts on her limbs. After her mother left, Claire entered the bathroom and examined her body for bruises. She saw none. Had she somehow eaten something poisonous? Her stomach didn't hurt. More bewildered than ever, her anxiety shooed sleep out the door for that night.

The next day a doctor visited. Dressed in a suit and tie, not a white coat, he said, "Miss King, I'm Doctor Carpenter. We're going to transfer you to another hospital for a few weeks until you feel better."

Weeks–no! she wanted to shout. There was nothing wrong with her. After she left, she resorted to sobs again. What about school? What about her friends, parties? Shopping?

That evening Etta and David both stopped by. "Mother, the doctor said I have to go to another hospital. For weeks!" She hicked a sob.

Etta looked at David. They thought it better not to tell her what she had done; it would be wiser if Claire learned of it under the psychiatrist's care.

"They need time to run some tests, Dear," David told her. "Don't worry about school, we'll send a tutor for you."

"Tests for what?" Claire wailed.

"The doctor will explain it when you get to the other hospital," Etta said. "Now you must rest, Dear, and don't worry."

Claire wanted to scream. She had never known such

frustration. Why wouldn't anyone tell her anything? After her parents left, she hurled the water pitcher at the wall, shattering it into a thousand bits.

The Ring

The day dawned in Chicago, blustery as usual. Hats, papers, and a few dried leaves competed in their races to fences and alleyways. People hunched against the wind, running for the trolley cars. David and Etta made the chilly journey from their apartment for supper at the Grand Pacific Hotel, where David had moved from the Palmer House while it underwent renovation.

Etta often wondered why David kept his suite at the hotel.

"For business," he said. His answer, however, raised the question about the nature of the business, especially when it required David being gone so often overnight.

While awaiting the meal, she began twirling her hair. David reached over and gently took her hand. He had grown accustomed to his lover's nervous habit but preferred she not display it in public.

"Etta, please," he whispered.

"Sorry, Darling," Etta murmured.

The couple's life together had taken on a semblance of

ordinariness, one day blending into another. Claire now resided in a psychiatric hospital, still recovering from her suicide attempt.

They finished their meal and were enjoying their steamy coffee. They had long ago decided the coffee at the Pacific to be the best in town.

David reached over again and took Etta's tiny hand in his.

"Darling, I have something I've been wanting to talk to you about." he said quietly.

Etta felt a horrid chill surge up her body, from her feet to her head. She had dreaded this day since the couple had become parents thirteen years ago. He's grown tired of me. He's weary of the lies he's told about his marital status, and anxious to get on with what he truly wants—a reputable life in society.

David reached into his vest pocket and pulled out the little black taffeta-covered square box with its rounded top from the jeweler.

I Do

The First Presbyterian Church of Chicago hosted the wedding of Etta and David. It turned out to be a beautiful affair, although sparsely attended by few friends of David's. Etta wore a lovely brown silk gown trimmed in Belgian lace and seed pearls; David wore black tie and tails, as his bride had always wanted a sunset wedding. Etta smiled up at Uncle Matthew as he took her arm to walk her down the aisle. No other Andrews family members attended. *The Tribune* posted a simple three-line notice of the wedding.

Church decorations consisted of sprays of cream-colored roses and baby's breath displayed on the ends of the first few pews. Tiffany vases of lilies stood erect on the altar like palace guards. Fragrant stephanotis perfumed the air, and ivory candles cast a romantic glow over the church. The chilly but fair day did not impinge on Etta's happiness.

Rev. Barnes smiled and nodded at the couple as he began the ceremony.

After the vows were said, the small party journeyed to the Palmer House, where a sumptuous feast awaited the guests who dined on 'Consomme printanier, Amandes Cele'ese, Pommes Parisianes, Canard de Tete' Rouge, Salade de Laitui, Gateaus assortis, and, of course, wedding cake. Uncle Matthew gave the toast, and the dancing lasted until the eastern sun swept the darkness off Lake Michigan.

The couple took no honeymoon as Claire, not yet home from the mental hospital, still needed her parents nearby. Etta dared not to go too far from the moody and depressed child after the debacle at the private school.

The following day, after awakening in the suite at the hotel, David said to Etta, "I have a wedding present for you."

Another gift! she thought. He had already given her a magnificent strand of large, creamy white pearls, which she wore with her wedding dress. "What is it, David," she asked, bursting with curiosity.

"You'll see, my Dear–but after breakfast. We'll have to travel a bit."

"I'm intrigued." She could hardly retain her excitement at the thought of yet another fine gift from her husband.

After a breakfast of cold salmon, fresh strawberries, and fluffy pancakes, the couple had the valet pack their bags and set out.

A fine day, unusual for December, greeted the couple with a light cool breeze and mild temperature, adding to their pleasurable train trip. The seventeen-mile trip to Riverside didn't seem long as the two laughed and talked, nuzzling one another as newlyweds do.

Upon arriving, David steered the carriage through ornate gates set in a stone wall, which made it difficult for Etta to see the house.

"Whoa," said David.

Once inside the walled area, Etta all but lost her breath at the sight of a large mansion.

"What is this, Dear?" she asked. "Where are we?"

"This is our new home," replied David.

Her own mansion! She nearly forgot to breathe as she stood in the open carriage staring at the facade—imposing stone, with wide brass-decked double doors, marble stairs, wrought-iron railings, and a welcoming wrap-around porch on the west side.

"How . . . what. . ." Etta stammered.

David took her hand and smiled. "Dearest Etta, the city has become nearly unlivable, as you must know. I thought we could join our friends out here in the country. It's a new start. . ." He stopped himself, then finished his sentence. "For both of us."

Etta and David joined other well-to-do Chicagoans who chose to relocate. The clean air and spaciousness of the country encouraged thousands of families to leave the city. The new train lines helped those who liked to be close to Chicago.

Coffee, Black

The day after their wedding, morning broke in Bradford Hall with alarming clarity, the crystal-clear air shimmering with the dawn. Etta sat up and looked around at her new surroundings.

"I've made it," she whispered to herself. "I've finally made it. I have everything I've ever dreamed of—marriage, a lovely home, and a family." and wealth, although she didn't whisper that aloud.

She lay back down with a sigh of contentment. Then she noticed something else. SILENCE. No street noises, clanging, horse hooves, or chatter. The last time she witnessed that lovely phenomenon was at thirteen when she had left her nana's farm in Pennsylvania for Pittsburgh. She arose and threw open the window, closed her eyes and inhaled the pure, sweet air.

She heard a light knock on her door. "Yes?"

A voice replied, "Breakfast, Missus Andrews."

Oh, this is just too much, she thought—her new marital status and breakfast in bed all in one morning.

"Come in."

"Good morning, Missus." said the maid Alice with a thick Irish brogue.

"Mister David asked that I bring your breakfast this morning. He's already left for the city."

How lovely! She and David had agreed that since Etta loved to cook, she would manage all the meals, so one prepared by another seemed a real treat.

David had hired two staff members to work for them. Alice, a recent immigrant from Ireland, who filled out her uniform with a rounded body and ruddy face, would be perpetually busy with twenty-two rooms to clean, laundry, picking up after Claire, and tending to other household duties. She had met her husband on the boat across the Atlantic and they married soon afterward. David charged her husband, Jessie, the groundskeeper, with the management of farming operations of the forty acres, care of the animals, and the machinery and house repairs. The two servants had rooms on the third floor and were off on Sundays.

"Thank you, Alice." said Etta. Alice placed the tray on her lap. It held broiled grapefruit with a maraschino cherry in the center, lovely browned French toast, two sunny eggs, and a small bowl of fresh berries with cream.

"I didn't know if you preferred coffee or tea, Ma'am," said Alice.

"Oh, coffee, please, Alice. No cream or sugar." The maid left to brew the beverage.

Etta sat back on the embroidered pillows. It just keeps getting better and better, she said to herself. Am I dreaming? But then remembered the wedding, the dinner, the wedding night at the Palmer House, and the train ride to Riverside.

I want this moment to last forever. I should get a ribbon or a trophy for finally accomplishing the goal I made back in the Andrews's kitchen fourteen years ago.

Etta didn't pray often, but whispered, "Thank you, God. Thank you, thank you."

Life in the Country

None of the rumors of her past life followed Etta into the suburbs. Local society accepted her and David-they were even befriended by a few couples from the city who had followed the popular trend of fleeing the chaotic urban throng.

Etta embraced the mantle of suburban life as easily as a feather falling onto a pond. The last item she added to the furnishings of Bradford Hall was the Corot painting from David's father's mansion Uncle Matthew had procured and given them as a wedding present. Once she decorated the house to her liking, she opened it for tours and donated the proceeds to charity.

The weekly luncheons she gave for the social elite became events everyone desired. She joined the local charity sewing committee, played whist once a week, did her obligatory volunteer work at a local hospital, and served on several women's groups' boards of directors. The couple gave generously to charity and joined the Episcopal Church.

Etta, living the life of her dreams, enrolled Claire in a good school nearby. As the child still went by Claire King, everyone assumed her father had died. No one questioned Claire or Etta about it. David spent nearly every night at home, and life was good.

Eastgate

One chilly evening in September, David announced that he had to make a trip to Kentucky. He would be gone several days. Etta missed him terribly–the house seemed so empty without him.

A few days later, Etta heard a clattering across the driveway and saw David unhitching a horse trailer. Down from it trotted a gorgeous jet-black American Saddlebred steed. David had missed riding for pleasure since he had left Virginia. She leaned on the white-painted fence in the rear yard and watched him put the steed through his paces.

"He's a beauty, David." Her husband looked so tall, confident, and elegant on his mount.

"Yes, I had to look quite a while to find him. I named him 'Eastgate,' after my uncle's estate in Kentucky." replied David. He looked more pleased than she had seen him in a while. All the stress and wear of being in competitive real estate that had etched itself into his face seemed now erased by the equine purchase. Etta wanted to climb the fence, snatch him off his mount and lead him to the bedroom. She giggled and told herself she'd better not take this moment of pleasure away from him for a moment of fun for her.

David mounted Eastgate, clicked his tongue and gave a him a gentle nudge. It was time the two became acquainted. After trotting a bit, David leaned forward and urged his horse into a full gallop. Flying across the fields to nowhere, rider and horse became familiar with one another as they became one. David's head neared the saddle as they cleared fences and streams.

"Whoa," David murmured and slowed Eastgate to a walk. Looking around the landscape, David thought, what a miracle we have wrought here. All about him lay the symbols of success of the early settlers of Illinois–barns, houses, fields bursting with green. Prosperity out of this endless bog of a state. David rarely thought of his own success–it was always taken for granted, inbred, almost. As he looked down at the giant colorful wild violets at his feet, he was suddenly so overtaken by gratitude tears came to his eyes. Overcome by a strong desire to be with his beloved, he turned the horse and headed home.

On the way, he realized he had lost his way. Spotting a small shed just ahead, he steered Eastgate towards it. "Hello, anyone there?" he called. Silence. Once again, this time louder as he looked around the property.

Just as he was about to leave, a young man, rag in hands, came out of the building. "May I help you, sir?" he asked, noticing the fine horse and apparel of the rider. "Are you here to place a cola order?"

"I seem to have lost my way."

Not too tall, sandy-haired with brilliant blue eyes, the man stopped cleaning his hands. "What are you looking for?"

"My family just moved into Bradford Hall," David replied.

"Oh, yes, I heard. Welcome to our little community." He pointed north-east and gave directions. David thanked him and set Eastgate to a trot.

Claire Acts Out

Bradford Hall had housed the Andrews for five years, and life was good. Claire, eighteen, had finished high school, was learning to 'be a lady,' and would soon make her debut. Etta was busy making the elaborate arrangements to be held at the Palmer House Hotel in December 1896. Claire would be descending the staircase with the best of Chicago's elite, due to take her place in society after eighteen years of living on the fringe. The mother and daughter had yet to choose the dress for the big day.

One unusually warm fall day, just a few weeks before the debut, Etta, engrossed in reading on the big wrap-around porch, rang for Alice to bring her a lemonade.

The porch served as her favorite spot as she could watch the sunsets, something denied her in Chicago due to the tall buildings. She had a stew simmering on the stove for supper. Moments later, Alice answered the summons with the requested beverage. "Here you are, Mrs. Andrews."

"How have you been, Alice, I haven't had a chance to talk to you in quite a while, we've both been so busy."

"Well, ma'am, everything is just wonderful. There's just one small problem I need to talk to you about." Alice looked at the floor, the silver tray still in her hand. The lemonade pitcher sparkled with cool, shiny dewdrops.

"What is it?" Etta laid her book aside, readjusted the decorative pillows, and turned in her wicker chair to face Alice.

"Well, Mrs. Andrews, I don't want to be a tattler, but Claire has done something that Jessie and I think you and the mister should know about."

"Yes?" The late afternoon sun splintered into the trees.

"Well, last Sunday, while you and Mr. Andrews were in the city, I came downstairs for some supper, and I couldn't find Claire."

"What do you mean?"

"Well, we couldn't find her anywhere. Jessie even looked all around the grounds and at the neighbors'. We were afraid she had been kidnaped, and tried to call you at the Palmer House, but there was no answer. Then we caught her sneaking back into the house after dark. We didn't say anything because we wanted to talk to you first."

Etta stared off at the sunset. She had feared leaving her rambunctious teenager with the help on their day off might lead to problems.

"Thank you so much for letting us know, Alice. I'll discuss it with David."

"Thank you, ma'am," said Alice." I hope I didn't cause a problem by telling you."

"No, absolutely not, Alice. I appreciate it very much. Mr. Andrews and I don't want you to have to worry about Claire on your days off."

Etta was livid but wouldn't confront Claire until David got home and they could discuss it.

Meeting Edward

The Andrews were adjusting well to country life. As much as Etta missed the bustle of the city, the quiet countryside had become her haven.

Soon after moving to Riverside, Etta had discovered a popular local soft drink bottled at a nearby spring and developed a weakness for its alleged healing powers. Once a week, she would send Alice to the small building where the Exton family bottled the cola.

Claire loved riding along, and, from the carriage, glimpsed a young man inside. She strained to see him through the dimly lit interior—not very tall but quite hand-some. One day he caught her eye and flashed her a smile, showing white, even teeth.

One crisp fall day, Claire jumped down from the carriage as the leaves waved colorful goodbyes to all passersby. "Never mind, Alice, I'll get it," she told her before the maid could alight.

Claire pretended to look around while sneaking fleeting glances at the young man inside. He caught her eye a couple of times and smiled a wide grin. He knew why she was there —and it had nothing to do with cola.

"May I help you, Miss?" Edward Exton queried as he sauntered over to her.

Claire found herself speechless—she stuttered—she mumbled. Seeing him close up had satisfied all her curiosity. He appeared even more handsome than he had looked in the gloomy interior.

She cleared her throat. "Well, I'm here to pick up the Andrews order."

"Oh, the family in Bradford Hall," he exclaimed.

"Yes, that's me. I mean, that's us. I mean that is correct." She cleared her throat again. "Our, or, their regular weekly order."

Edward looked amused. He could tell by her dress she wasn't a servant. She must be the daughter of the house.

All of Riverside talked about the family renting Bradford Hall. Some folks said the renter's father had served as governor of Virginia, and others that they were one of the wealthiest families in Chicago.

Edward had yet to pay much attention to the gossip about the Andrews family. When not helping out his grandfather at the spring, he spent his time with his father, tinkering with their inventions in the Riverside family home basement. But when Edward saw Claire, bells rang. He'd never been in love, so the feelings were entirely new– and he liked them.

Over the next few weeks, Claire slipped into the facility as often as possible. One day Edward invited Claire deeper into the facility to see how they bottled the cola. She feigned interest, but her thoughts were about being alone with him. He suddenly pushed her against a wall pressing his body against hers; Claire felt faint.

He gazed at her, then slowly pressed his lips against hers in her first kiss. She trembled with passion–or fear?

The weekly visits paused when winter arrived, bringing snowy roads. Claire pressed Alice into smuggling the young couple's letters by post to one another. Again and again, Edward professed his love for Claire. When Etta locked her errant daughter in the servant's quarters to keep her close on weekends, his words of love gave her strength, even resolve.

She wrote him about how cruelly her mother treated her and how distant her father seemed. She expressed her pain at being bullied at Girls' Normal School and dropping out. She now remembered her attempt on her own life but didn't mention it. She dreaded her looming coming-out event. "Coming out! Coming out of what? Makes me sound like a birthing cow!" she wrote. "I would rather have a tooth pulled!"

Finally, Edward proposed.

"We can't marry, you know that!" exclaimed Claire, denying the butterflies in her stomach.

"We can elope."

Claire was stunned. She had never thought of that.

"How? When? Where?" she replied.

The pair hatched a plan to run away the next weekday Claire's parents were in Chicago. She stole a pair of earrings from her mother's jewelry box and pressed them into Alice's hand. "Please, Alice, just look the other way if you hear anything tomorrow." Her pleading brown eyes touched Alice. The maid nodded.

Alice took the earrings from her pocket and looked down at them—rubies surrounded by diamonds in a teardrop design. The temptation of owning such a treasure won, and a week later, at eleven a. m., Alice Butler went downstairs and started the noisy dishwasher as soon as she heard someone behind the house.

Edward, clutching a map of the rear of the house drawn by Claire, showing the location of the rear of Bradford Hall, left his carriage about a quarter mile down the road. He silently crept toward the huge house and, picking up a rock, knocked it softly on the driveway three times, the code for their alliance. A moment later, Claire quietly joined him.

Edward and Claire were married in Waukegan by a Justice of the Peace on November 20, 1896.

The News

Etta snapped the whip at her horse, eager to get home. The funeral of David's friend, Abner Scott, had been heavily attended by Chicago's elite. Abner, David's neighbor at the Palmer House, had died from a fall from his fourth-floor balcony. After the funeral, David stayed in the city for business.

Etta had told Alice to lock Claire in the spare servants' bedroom again for the night. Braced for the temper tantrums, the slammed doors, and silence for days upon her return, Etta hoped that, after her societal debut, Claire would find a suitable suitor for her tempestuous rebel to marry and tame her. Perhaps a houseful of screaming children will do the trick—yet she and David had not yet found time to discuss Claire's weekend escapades. She had been preoccupied with getting ready for their fifh Thanksgiving at Bradford Hall and was looking forward to a hot bath.

Etta sighed and turned the carriage into the wide driveway. A stranger stood by his mount in front of the house.

What does he want? She hated salesmen coming to the house and usually sent Jessie to deal with them.

"Whooah," she said.

"Mrs. Andrews?" the man approached her. He looked like a country local, with poor clothes and an unkempt appearance. "I'm Howard Exton, a cousin of Edward Exton."

Etta stared at him. Who was Edward Exton? She had never heard of him. Why is this man here?

"Well?" she asked impatiently.

"Ma'am," the man looked down at the cobblestones as he shifted back and forth, nervously turning his hat round and round in his hands. "I was sent here by my cousin to give you some news."

"Yes?" Now Etta was curious. Had the cow she sold last week died? Was he a creditor after David?

"Well," he said again. He coughed and shuffled his feet.

Etta, still seated on the carriage, was losing patience. "Well, WHAT?" she demanded.

The man flinched at her tone. "I'm here to tell you that your daughter and Edward Exton done got married while you was away."

"WHAT," Etta screamed, standing erect in the carriage, the whip still in her hand. The horse whinnied and reared.

"Yes, ma'am. They done eloped Friday. At Lake County." He stepped closer. Edward had told him he might expect a tip.

It took a moment for this news to register in Etta's mind. Rage flooded in like a red tsunami, and without thinking, she raised her whip straight at Howard Exton.

The papers were all over the story. Matthew stayed in the city when it made the front page of *The Chicago Tribune*.

Rant

Etta strode through the house, ranting and raving. Alice ran from the kitchen, alarmed at all the yelling.

Jessie dashed outside to help the screaming man. "What happened?" he asked the stranger, writhing on the paving stones.

"Gee bwoke ma gsaw!" the man yelled. "Gee cwazy!"

"What? I can't understand you! What happened?"

The injured man pointed to the house. "GEE BWOKE MA GSAW."

Jessie didn't know what to do. He looked around to see if there were witnesses or someone to help. Obviously, the man's jaw was misaligned. He took out his handkerchief, wrapped the jaw, now reddening from the slash, helped the man up on his horse, and led them to the road. "Get to a doctor!" he yelled, slapping the horse's flank. Howard nearly fell off the horse, trying to lead it with one hand and holding his jaw with the other, but managed to right himself and set out.

Etta tried calling David on the telephone, but there was no answer. "I'm going to kill him," she shouted.

"Kill who?" the alarmed Alice asked. She had no idea what had happened, as Jessie hadn't yet come inside to tell her.

"The monster who kidnaped my daughter," yelled Etta. "I'm going to kill him."

"Ma'am," said Alice quietly, her hand gently on her employer's shoulder. "Why don't we sit down? I'll make you tea, and you can tell me all about it."

That quieted Etta a bit.

"Let's go out on the porch. I'll bring your tea and a fresh scone."

The idea of food often took precedence over everything else to Etta, so she stepped out on the sunny side porch and sat down, fitfully rocking back and forth, muttering to herself.

Alice brought her tea and cinnamon scone, freshly baked by Alice herself, who occasionally took a turn in the kitchen. She pulled up a chair.

"Now ma'am, tell me what happened."

Jessie arrived on the porch and shook his head at his wife. Alice wasn't sure what he meant, so she rubbed Etta's arm and pleaded to tell her what had just transpired.

"Claire's been kidnaped." Etta then broke down in shoulder-shattering sobs. Alice jerked back.

"She what?" She looked at her husband to get more information. Jessie remained silent.

The maid had difficulty understanding Etta because of her sobbing. "My daughter–my only precious child–has been kidnaped by some yokel."

Alice and Jessie continued giving one another glances. Living in such evident luxury always brought the specter of kidnaping to every well-off family, which caused many to downplay their fortunes, dressing down in public and keeping their names out of the newspapers. Of course, Alice knew about the elopement, as she had been an accomplice.

Etta finally calmed down enough to sip her tea. She didn't know what to do and needed to confer with David, but unable to reach him, she spent the rest of the day sputtering, pacing, and sobbing.

The Press

It didn't take long for the local press to catch wind off the incident. Before long, reporters from all over the county—even Chicago—had staked out in the circular driveway of Bradford Hall. Jessie stood at the front door to try to fend them off.

Their shouts of, "What happened, Mrs. Andrews?" and, "Has your daughter been kidnaped?" rang across the paving stones. Etta had retreated to a rear room with a glass of bourbon. She had been unable to reach David, his telephone ringing again and again each time she called.

She finally could wait no longer and called the sheriff and convinced him to have a warrant sworn out for Edward Exton's arrest. Her daughter's life might be at stake, she maintained. She prayed Claire wasn't being tortured or raped. She pressed the back of her hand on her forehead and moaned, "my poor baby!"

Etta's mind would not accept that her daughter had willingly let herself be taken. She suspected a conspiracy between her mansion help and Edward Exton. After all,

Claire was locked in the third-floor servants' quarters. How else could she have gotten out?

Suddenly a movement behind her caught her attention. A man with a camera peered through her window. She ran over, opened it, and gave him a hard shove. Fortunately, he landed on a boxwood hedgerow when he went flying. He did not appear hurt, but his box camera met its end when it shattered upon hitting the pebbled back driveway.

Etta screamed at the top of her voice. She could not imagine what would happen next as if she didn't have enough to worry about without trespassers. And the thought hit her--what will David think when he hears the news? A shock of dread pulsed through her body. He'll be furious at the publicity. After all, the dear man had worked so hard, taking Etta and Claire out of the lives they had been living, moving them to the suburbs, and investing heavily in obtaining them socially acceptable lives.

Etta had something more significant to consider than her daughter's errant behavior. She stood a good chance of losing everything.

And Now to Jail

The next day, Edward Exton and his new bride Claire were enjoying an afternoon of marital bliss when the sheriff banged on his parents' door where the couple lived.

"Open up, police," he shouted. Edward sat up in bed, glanced at Claire, then quickly put on his pants and ran down the stairs.

"Sheriff? What is it?"

The expression on the sheriff's face told Edward this wasn't a social call.

"You're under arrest, Edward."

Edward thought he must have been dreaming. He had known the sheriff all his life.

"Wh ... what?"

The sheriff grabbed Edward's arm and pulled him outside.

" 'm arresting you for the kidnaping of Claire Walker," he stated.

"Wait! Sheriff. You don't understand-we were married

yesterday, in Lake County- have the document to prove it."

"That's not what hear," answered the sheriff. "Her mother has had a warrant put out for your arrest-she says you kidnaped her daughter."

Claire appeared behind her husband in her dressing gown and leaned against his back as though to protect him. "Ask her," said Edward, jerking his hand over his shoulder and pointing to Claire.

His bride, her hair in disarray and barefoot, wrapped her arms around her husband's waist. "What are you doing?" she cried to the sheriff.

" 'm arresting this man for your kidnaping. Ma'am, you all right?"

"Of course am all right! 'm on my honeymoon! Now go, and leave us alone!"

"Well, have to let the court decide. have a warrant for his arrest. 'm taking this man in. Now."

Claire backed away as the sheriff led her groom to the Cook County Jail, where he would remain for several days.

A week later, after failing to get her daughter to return home, Etta appeared at the hearing, dressed in her finest black silk to emphasize her status and grief.

When Edward entered the courtroom, Etta got her first look at him and recognized him from the cola factory. He, indeed, was very handsome-more to lead a young girl astray -she thought. Her hatred burned like hot coals in her chest.

Etta had brought in an expensive attorney whose imposing dress and stature emphasized his status in the courtroom.

"Are all the plaintiffs here?" asked the Judge.

"No, sir, the chief plaintiff, Mr. David Andrews has not yet arrived."

"We'll give him fifteen minutes," replied the Judge.

Etta sat in the front row, twisting her black lace gloves. Where is David? He had agreed to the arrest when she had finally reached him in the city.

David tendered terse replies when she explained what had happened on the telephone a few days before the hearing. He made her aware of the scandal the jaw-breaking incident had created in the Chicago newspapers. David sounded furious-she could tell by his tone. Etta had never felt so vulnerable or regretful in how she had lost her temper. t seemed she'd begun to gain some control for the past few years, but now she realized there were fewer occasions in her new life to lose it.

The fifteen minutes were over. The Judge dismissed the court, and the charges were dropped. Edward gave Etta a long look as he left the courtroom. She felt humiliated. She knew she looked like a fool to the whole town.

Residue

News traveled fast in the small community of Riverside. The elopement did not depend upon newspapers to bring scandal to the public's attention. Of course, David's failure to attend the hearing made the front pages of the major Chicago newspapers. He remained absent from Bradford Hall for two weeks.

Etta's social life came to a sudden and complete halt. No one came to tour the house. Etta and David no longer received luncheon invitations or social calls from friends. When she went into town, people seemed to step out of their way to avoid her. Society dropped the Andrews family like a used opera flyer blown into a corner of an alley.

When David did return home, the change in him sent chills down Etta's spine. Her temper had finally destroyed everything they had worked so hard building together.

"Hello, Dear." she smiled weakly.

No hug. No kiss. No warm greeting. No eye contact. David set down his briefcase and sat in the big brown leather chair.

"We'll be moving back to the city." He didn't look up.

Etta slumped in a nearby chair. There's nothing I can say. At least he's said nothing about divorce. But she couldn't help but wonder if she could ever restore any of the happiness she had enjoyed with her lover.

A week later, Etta stood at the long front window of Bradford House, tears streaming down her face, watching David lead 'Eastgate' onto a horse trailer to be transported to his new owner. The guilt swept through her body like an unwelcome fever. Nothing will ever be the same again.

The Future

Etta moved into a small apartment in Chicago. David had moved back to the Palmer House and stayed with her even less than before the move. Their social life was as dismal as a city back alley. Etta again sank into depression and rarely went out—half-hearted painting, puttering in the tiny garden in the rear, and baking filled her empty days.

After her daughter's elopement, Etta couldn't find her favorite pair of ruby earrings. After she reported the theft to the police, the papers again churned with the Andrews name. The couple she had employed had disappeared–most likely joining the surge of immigrants to the West.

She remembered the old seer one cool fall day and decided to call on her. In a way, she dreaded showing up under her cloud of defeat. Madam Vertina probably already knew much, if not all, of that from what the news media had reported.

She decided to walk. She needed fresh air and time to think and now lived nearer the gypsy's poorer neighborhood.

She knocked. Madam Vertina opened the door.

"Etta! Good to see you! How you been? Come!"

Etta entered, and the mystic could see her crestfallen manner.

"Please, sit," the old woman directed. Etta had forgotten about her strong Romanian accent.

"Thank you, Madam."

A new paisley scarf lay on the table, but little else had changed since Etta's last visit. The room seemed stuffy and oppressive.

"I've ruined everything." Etta murmured. She explained to the old woman all that had happened since she last saw her, frequently stopping to dab her tears. "What is to become of me, of my life?"

"We ask cards." said Madam.

She brought out the Tarot cards and went through them, turning each over with the care of an archeologist cleaning an artifact.

"Change coming soon," she murmured. "Your life be filled with joy and grandchildren. Reconciliation will come. You find happiness again."

When she got to the last card, she turned it over, glanced at it, then at Etta, who hadn't noticed it. She quickly hid it in her lap.

Reconciliation

Etta sat, rocking, by the window in the small apartment. The sky had turned dark, and the rumbling of the storm added to her mood. After she turned on a lamp and lit a fire in the fireplace, she walked over to the buffet and struggled to open the bottom drawer. She sighed. The humid weather had caused the drawer to stick again. After tugging it open, she reached under a stack of papers, pulled out a fabric-covered box, and returned to her chair. Where was it? She was sure she had saved it. Her past life marched in front of her in print as she leafed through concert programs, invitations, news clippings, and dance cards—decades of memories relegated to a graveyard in a stuck drawer.

The item lay at the box's very bottom—the escort card Billy Black had given her at the Fourth of July dance so many years ago. She lay her head on the back of the rocker, tea chilling in its cup. She thought, this was the little card that started me on this journey. An unexpected twist in the road and an unplanned life led me to this chair—a rich life, now as hollow as a punched balloon. Maybe I should get another cat.

She shuffled to the wardrobe in her slippers, robe ties dragging behind her to put another log on the fire. Over the past few years, her love of food had begun showing around her waist. The temperature had dropped. Suddenly a loud rap at the front door made her jump. Who could that be on this awful night? The storm raged, and when Etta peered out into the darkness, she was shocked. A woman stood on the stoop, soaked and dripping, with two small sobbing children in tow.

"Mother?"

Etta jumped back, struggling to hold the door open against the wind.

"Claire? What are you doing here?" Etta's anger had eased since Claire's elopement, and her daughter's appearance moved the grandmother.

"I've left Edward, and have no where else to go," cried Claire. "And can you pay the taxi? I have no money." A cab sat waiting at the curb, engine running.

The mother and daughter had not been in contact for six years. Etta had missed the births of her granddaughter Henrietta—her four-year-old namesake—and a two-year-old boy named after Etta's alleged husband, Charles.

Etta ushered them in, grabbed dry towels, added a log to the fire, and put a kettle of water on to boil. She dried and calmed the children while listening to Claire tell her story.

"Edward came home drunk again and began yelling and throwing things around our small bedroom. The children were terrified, so I decided I had enough. I packed them up, took the train into the city, and here I am."

She began to sob. Etta felt her daughter's fear and pain

and stood clumsily, embracing her shaking shoulders. She didn't know what to say. *Should I call David? He would know what to do.* After cups of hot cabbage soup and crackers, the children fell asleep, so the women moved them to Etta's bedroom and again took their seats in the parlor.

Etta took a long look at her daughter. She had matured—looked older and more worn. "You can stay here as long as you need," Etta told her. "David will help you out. We'll call him in the morning. How did you find me?"

"I looked your address up in the telephone directory at the train station," replied Claire.

"Are you still living with your in-laws?"

"Yes, unfortunately. We have no money nor is there any coming in. Edward's dad is as crazy as his son, with his patents and all. The pair spend all their time in the basement tinkering, banging their latest creations into wooden boxes, and shipping them off to Washington for patent approval. There's never a moment's peace."

Etta remembered how she loved the quiet of the country at Bradford Hall. *What a shame,* she thought.

Claire and Etta sipped their tea. "They are both inventors, you know," Claire said, munching on a lemon and poppy seed muffin.

"Inventors of what?"

"Oh, I don't know, um—his dad invented a piece for organs—reeds—or something, and he made some wire with spiky things attached that's supposed to keep livestock from getting out of their pens."

"Have they profited from their inventions?" Etta questioned.

"Oh, my goodness, not a penny!" Claire said with a chortle. "Apparently, inventiveness isn't necessarily accompanied by business sense!" The women chuckled, pondering what had just been said. The storm raged outside. Claire shivered at the sound.

"His family was one of the first to settle in Riverside," Claire told her. "His grandfather founded the company that made the cola you liked so much when we lived there. Do you remember that?"

Etta nodded as the memories came flooding back like a tidal wave.

"He–his grandfather—worked as an attorney from Massachusetts before moving to Illinois, and *his* grandfather fought for the Revolution. The Exton family arrived from England around 1632. With the Windsor fleet," she added. Claire droned the facts as though reciting for her sixth-grade class, looking at the floor, recalling her early days with her husband's family, listening to their ancestral tales. "One day, Edward's grandfather, after drinking from a spring, found his rheumatism had improved. So he began bottling the water, claiming its healing powers."

Etta remembered the cola and the factory and nodded. So that's how they met, she thought.

Hearing these tidbits about the Exton family softened Etta's heart a bit. But she still could not forgive Edward for stealing her only child, especially now that Claire had to deal with him as a drunk, a dreamer, and a ne'er-do-well.

The women continued talking long into the night while the storm engaged in a frenzied tango with the trees, punctuated by shuddering claps of thunder. Neither woman mentioned the last time they had spoken when Claire had eloped six years ago.

As the children enjoyed breakfast the following day, little Henrietta gently poked her mother. "What shall we call her?" she whispered.

Etta overheard and chuckled. "You can call me 'Nonny,' " she suggested.

Henrietta squirmed in her chair with satisfaction. "All right, Nonny." She whispered the directions to her little brother, who looked up and nodded.

Claire had taken her coffee to the parlor. A small white card on a tri-legged table drew her attention. She picked it up and read it.

"May I Have the Pleasure of Seeing You Home Tonight?
If so, keep this card; if not, return it."

She turned it over. In clumsy script letters was the signature, 'Billy Black.'

"Mother?" she called back to the kitchen. "Mother, what is this?"

Etta slowly walked toward her daughter. The children's laughter dominated the scene, freezing the moment forever in Claire's mind.

"Well?" she asked, holding up the card.

A shock ran through Etta's chest. She thought, is now the time to tell her?

"Claire, I have a story to tell you."

Claire sat immobile as Etta relayed the tale of Billy Black, her alias as the widow of Charles King, life at the bordello, and the facts surrounding her daughter's birth.

Claire sat back with a plop, her eyes wide. "So Claire King is not even my real name?" Her face twisted into something Etta did not recognize. "And David really is my father?"

Etta reached over and took her daughter's hand. She lowered her eyes and nodded. "I've never been with anyone else."

Claire sat in stunned silence. All those years, all those lies. She glanced over at her children, now getting restless at the table.

"Who else knows?"

"No one. I'm not even sure David is convinced—after all. I had been moved upstairs at the bordello for a few weeks. Who would believe..." her voice trailed.

Claire sat across the table from David. He had come from the Palmer House when Etta reached him by telephone. Etta had taken the children to the zoo so father and daughter could be alone.

"Mother told me everything... Father," she called him for the first time, but, it seemed to David, said with a sharp tone. He lowered his head. So that is what Etta is saying, he thought. He wished he could be as confident as his wife. How can she be so sure? At times in the past, he had believed he had fathered Claire, but other times doubt overtook him.

"Father?" Claire interrupted his reverie. He would do the right thing as he did that December night when he walked along the beach after the Palmer House dinner. And she does look like me; he thought as he looked at Claire's face with her Andrews eyes, staring and full of questions.

"So, yes, it is all true." David responded. He reached across the table for her hand. "I'm so sorry, Darling," he whispered. "We were afraid of what people would say. It would have been the end of me, my business."

Claire drew back. "If you married?" she said, a sob

catching in her throat. She rose, knocking the chair over. "Do you have the slightest notion of what you put me through by not marrying? The shame, the bullying–my attempt on my own life?"

David arose and again reached out to her.

"No! Don't touch me!" she shouted, verging on hysteria. "Stay away! I never want to see you again. Get out," she yelled, moving toward him threateningly.

David backed away, grabbing his raincoat as he headed toward the door. His parting words, "Darling, I am so sorry," hung like a foul odor in the air.

Guilt overwhelmed him. *How could I have been so blind, so selfish!* Riddled with remorse, he knew he could never repair the damage he had heaped on his daughter's head–not in a lifetime. Hands in pockets, head down, he turned toward his hotel, needing to walk out his shame. He felt exposed, as he neglected to take his hat. He walked along the lake. But physical steps could never mend the rift that just ripped through their lives. By the time he reached Lincoln Park, he understood that. He sat on a bench and stared out at the water. The waves roiled against the sand —never slowing, never stopping, Omnipresent, like his guilt.

When Etta arrived home from the zoo with the children late that afternoon, she met a sorry sight. Her daughter quaked with rage.

"Mommy, Mommy!" Little Henrietta shouted. as she ran toward her mother. "We saw a tiger! A real tiger!"

Etta, concerned about Claire's state of mind, pulled her away. "Children, I have cream in the ice box. Now run wash up and I'll get some for you."

Etta didn't have to ask her daughter what had happened. She had feared Claire might confront her father about his past cowardice. The pair sat silent as the children chattered and enjoyed Etta's homemade peach ice cream.

Crushed by what had happened, Etta felt like the wind had left her. One relationship healed, another shattered, she thought.

The following two weeks flew by as 'Nonny' introduced the children to some of the city's joys—Riverview Park for the rides, swimming at the beach, and lunch at St. Elmo's. Etta truly spoiled them. Little Charlie growled like a lion and leaped at people for hours after the zoo visit. David busied himself trying to find a suitable apartment for them nearby. Of course, he would support them; they could be his offspring.

Claire realized she was pregnant again after just a few weeks in the city.

"Mother," she said one morning, "I have to go back."

"Why, Claire?"

Claire flushed with embarrassment. After all the terrible things she had heard about her son-in-law, Etta realized the couple had certain positive aspects in their relationship. And now, with their third child on its way, Claire had nowhere to go, just like her grandmother Mary Claire back in Pennsylvania when she found she was pregnant with Etta.

Etta's disappointment wiped out her joy like an old dusty eraser. She loved having the trio with her as her loneliness had dissipated with their arrival.

The drunken scene repeated itself just a few days after Claire's return. This time, she took matters into her own hands. No more running, she told herself—no more upheaval to my children's lives.

Once again, the sheriff again knocked on the Exton family's front door. The sheriff gazed at the colorful pansy boxes on the porch while waiting for a reply. It was spring, just a few months before Claire's baby Amy's birth.

Edward answered. His stomach dropped.

"What is it, Norm," he asked, using the sheriff's first name.

"I'm afraid it's worse this time, Ed," the sheriff replied, head down. "We have a court order to have you committed."

"You can't do that!" the shocked Ed yelled.

"Of course we can, that's why we're here. Your wife says you are a danger to her and the children. Now please step out."

Ed stepped back, the sheriff forward, grabbing his arm. "No monkey business, now, Ed, this is serious."

One hour later, Edward was admitted to the Illinois Eastern Hospital for the Insane.

One crisp golden day in October, Etta called Claire. "How is your husband doing?"

"Mother, I have the most beautiful letters from him nearly daily. He is such a dear while he is confined and not drinking, but I know if I tell them to release him, things will return to madness in just a few days. The bottle is always there, like an unwelcome visitor."

Etta had no experience with addictions, so she couldn't advise her daughter.

"Whatever you think is best," she advised. "You always have to think of the children."

Failure

David and Etta sat at the dining room table, finishing their coffee. Neither spoke. David had tried repeatedly to reconnect with Claire, even at her home in Riverside, but she refused to come out. When the door opened, he recognized the person who stood there—the young man who had helped him find his way home the day he was lost with Eastgate. So that's how they met. He slowly walked back to his car, his guilt again crushing.

Claire bore another daughter named Amy, after her mother's middle name. But two years later, Claire would receive devastating news on the telephone.

Papa Beckons

Ten days after Etta and David celebrated their sixteenth anniversary as an officially wed couple, they sat enjoying a sumptuous meal at the Grand Pacific. It was December 1910. Although their lives were vastly different, as when they were in Riverside, the couple had reached a place of acceptance with one another and their life back in the city.

The next morning, Etta rolled over in bed. She dreamt she had been kicked in the stomach by David's thoroughbred, 'Eastgate.' The sun slanted across the room, scooting the darkness into the corners. As she awoke, she realized the pain in her abdomen had not evaporated with the dream. She put her hand to her side and pressed gently.

"OW!" she cried aloud. David had left for work. The apartment was empty except for the day maid, Bonnie, another young Irish girl with a sunny disposition. Etta arose and went to the bathroom. She had regular movements nearly every day of her life, but this morning, nothing happened.

Throughout the day, the pain in her side increased. She

had Bonnie call the doctor. Etta heard his car pull up a couple of hours later. Bonnie led him into the bedroom.

"Good morning, Mrs. Andrews," he greeted her. "What seems to be the problem?"

"I have a horrid pain in my right side. And I can't go to the bathroom. It began early this morning, and it is getting worse."

He palpated her abdomen.

"It must be the grippe. Drink lots of fluids and call me in the morning."

"Doctor," Etta said, "Wait—I haven't had a movement today. That is very unusual for me."

"Well, that's not so unusual for the grippe," he stated. "We'll talk about it tomorrow."

The next day Etta continued writhing in agony. The pain had kept sleep at bay throughout the night. David stayed at his hotel so he wouldn't be exposed to the flu. Etta began vomiting and still had no bowel movement.

Etta called him. "David," she pleaded. "Please make sure the doctor comes around today."

David hated seeing her suffer but believed the doctor knew his trade.

"Yes, Dear, I will call and remind him. Now rest." He hung up the phone.

Cold, gloom, and wintry weather accompanied the doctor the next morning. He shook the snow off his hat and sat down beside Etta. Lowering the covers, he felt her abdomen again.

"I'm still in agony, Doctor." Etta pleaded. The water glass and decanter remained on the bedside table untouched. "I'm not able to keep even a sip of water down. And I can't sleep—the pain never stops." The doctor noticed she looked a bit haggard.

"Well, this grippe is bad," Dr. Morgan said, shaking his head. "I've been all over the city treating folks with it."

"But doctor, I still haven't had a movement." Why isn't he listening to me?

"Well, Etta, as you haven't been able to keep anything down, that's not so unusual. Your bowels will return to normal when you begin eating again. I'll stop by in the morning."

Etta still wasn't satisfied with his answer. She knew her body and felt death's icy breath on her neck. She groaned and turned away, settling back into her pain.

The pain felt like nothing she had ever experienced. Localized on her right side, it brought agony every minute, day and night. There was no respite or chance to catch her breath, as she could when in labor with Claire. When she could doze off, her dreams of thirst took her to deserts, staggering toward perceived, then vanishing, oases in the distance.

On the fourth day of Etta's misery, she wretched, and the contents lay in the bowl at the side of her bed, a silent witness to the reality of her condition. Later that morning, when the Doctor stopped by, he became alarmed when he looked at the bowl. It consisted of solid matter. He turned pale.

"I think you might need to get to the hospital." he said, clearing his throat. He dreaded thinking he had made an incorrect diagnosis. "Let me drive you there myself."

Etta leaned against the Doctor's arm as they left for the hospital. She felt frail. Etta didn't know it then but had lost twenty pounds in the past four days. Bonnie stared as her employer pointed to imagined cracks in the walls on the way out the door, saying, "The landlord needs to fix those."

The doctor leaned toward Bonnie and whispered,

"She's dehydrated." Dr. Morgan bundled his patient into his white Austin Touring car and set off for Baptist Hospital.

By the time the personnel had settled Etta in her room, she had become delirious. Her tongue stuck to the roof of her mouth, caused by the dehydration. Her cracked and dry lips had lost any color.

A nurse came into the room with a needle.

"Mrs. Andrews?" she asked. Etta grunted. "We're preparing you for surgery. In the meantime, this will make you feel better."

Etta rolled over so the nurse could administer the palliative. She felt a lovely warmth take over her body in just a few seconds. It wasn't unlike the tea that the gypsy woman had given her. The pain flew away like a white dove. Etta slept and dreamt of being on the farm.

Etta felt a hand gently jostling her foot. She forced herself awake, wondering if the nurse was coming to administer more nirvana.

"Papa?" she spoke. "What are you doing here?" Smiling, standing at the foot of the bed, he looked young enough to be her son. She tried to clear her eyes and brain of the fog. Objects had no outlines, borders, or definitions, like coffee spilled on a fresh watercolor painting.

The apparition smiled. "I've come to take you home. It's time." He reached out for her.

She placed her bare feet on the cold floor but did not feel the chill. She took her father's hand.

The Mausoleum

David stood, head bowed, in front of Etta's crypt at the mausoleum at Oak Hill Cemetery. Looking down at the marble floor, he recalled the first day he met her at Martha Webster's. How naive she had been—that we both had been.

He raised his head and read the engraving on her vault.

'Henrietta Amy Andrews, 1858-1910.'

The pair had enjoyed thirty beautiful years together, and now she was gone. David had never felt so alone. Etta's love had helped him endure subtle rejection by his family and the isolation he had felt all those years not quite being a member of the Andrews clan. The clang of a nearby crypt door slamming shut reminded him of the purpose of his visit. He placed the white roses on the cold floor.

"Goodbye, my Love; God bless you and keep you." he whispered.

David wasn't particularly religious but felt these words

were the best he could come up with. It had been his thirtieth visit to the site in as many weeks.

He hadn't been able to be with Etta when she closed her eyes for the last time and had never forgiven himself. He was involved in a deal that meant quite a bit of money, and he believed Etta would be coming home from the hospital soon. He had been in the final phase of the business transaction when he got the call at his office.

"Mr. Andrews?" A male voice said. "This is Doctor Morgan. Are you sitting down? I'm afraid I have some bad news. I regret to tell you that your wife has passed away."

David didn't move. Had he heard correctly? "Excuse me?" he asked.

"At three o'clock this afternoon. I'm so sorry we were not able to save her. We tried to call you, but there was no answer."

"What?" David couldn't process the Doctor's words. Am I in a dream—or nightmare? He looked over at his client. "Could you excuse me for a moment?" he asked. The man nodded and stepped out.

"What happened?" asked David of the doctor.

"Your wife suffered from an intestinal obstruction," answered Dr. Morgan. "It was quite advanced when she arrived here. There was nothing we could do. She died on the operating table."

"What is that?" David choked.

"It seems your wife's small intestine got entangled upon itself, causing a stoppage of the blood flow. Unfortunately, gangrene set in."

David sat down with a plop. I can't believe it! And I trusted that doctor implicitly! He finished his business transaction in a fog.

There is so much to do. The cremation. And the

funeral; how to handle that? He decided to place a perfunctory notice in the city papers. He didn't want to begin answering long-held questions at the service about his marriage or Claire's parentage with a lengthy obituary. Suddenly, he realized he hadn't told Claire. He picked up the phone.

Claire's Reaction

Claire answered the telephone.

"Claire, don't hang up!" David shouted. Claire hesitated. "Your mother is dead!"

His daughter screamed. The ear receiver dangled from its cord, banging against the wall in the tiny hall in Riverside. It had been two years since she had spoken to her father.

"Mother is dead." She dropped to the floor, saying it over and over. As chaotic as their relationship had been, Etta had been her mother and a wonderful grandmother to the three small children.

The children gathered around her, eyes wide, not knowing what to say. Finally, Henrietta, six, said, "Mama, is Nonny dead?"

Claire began wailing again, her tears making rivulets in the creases of her blouse.

Little Henrietta walked over to her and put her arms around her mother. "Mama, please don't cry." Amy began to wail, and Charlie just watched. He had often seen his mother behave erratically, but he hadn't seen this type of hysteria before. He wasn't sure about death. He just knew people went someplace and didn't come back. He wondered if it was like his toy soldier in the backyard, under several inches of snow and mud. He had just made his Christmas letter to Santa and had asked for a new one. He doubted Santa could bring it because his soldier was dead.

Claire sat up, taking Henrietta in her arms. "Oh, Darlings, your beloved Nonny has gone to live with Jesus."

After making the necessary arrangements, Claire packed her valise. She was fortunate to still live with her in-laws, who were constant and outstanding babysitters. She broke down again between every pair of bloomers and blouses she packed. Why had she been such a horrid daughter, missing out on all those years with her parents? Now she would never be forgiven!

Her husband, Edward, did not attend the funeral.

Visiting Matthew

Two years later David steered his new 1912 Empire Runabout onto the highway toward Oak Park and the old folks' home. The drive awakened many memories of when that neighborhood, now a suburb of Chicago, was in the country. So much had changed—the new century had turned the Windy City into one of the country's largest and most prosperous urban areas. Huge parks and wide roads had kicked aside the nasty odors and filth, and leafy trees grew alongside the art-deco skyscrapers that sprouted up like spring dandelions.

The chair's wheels squeaked as David pushed Uncle Matthew onto the expansive lawn. The elderly man had outlived his brother James by twenty-eight years, and the years were showing on his face and body. David picked a place under a large oak tree and chose a bench across from him.

"Uncle, how are you feeling?"

Matthew laughed. His palsied hands were shaking as he spoke. "Well, it's not so bad being here, especially if you consider the alternative," he said jokingly. He had not lost his sense of humor. "The food is not so bad, and I am mad about my young nurse."

David chuckled, glad to see the uncle he knew in his youth was still present.

"How have you been?" Matthew asked, pulling the cashmere blanket closer over his bony knees and leaning slightly toward David.

"Well, thank you Uncle, but I must say..." he hesitated. "I miss her more than I ever thought possible. But I am seeing someone..."

"Anyone I know?" asked Matthew.

"You may—Marion McCarthy? Do you remember her? Her family had the box seat next to ours at the opera."

Matthew nodded. "Yes, I do, Son. A fine lady. I'm happy to hear that. It's hard being alone." He paused. "Hmmm. Catholic. You'll convert?"

David lowered his head and twirled his thumbs, saying, " Yes, she's good for me."

Matthew said, "How is the family?" referring to Claire and her children.

"Wonderful." said David. "Being a grandfather is one of the greatest joys of my life." He stopped, realizing Matthew and his wife were never blessed with children. After marrying late in life, his wife died after only ten years of marriage.

"I'm sorry, Uncle."

"That's all right," said Matthew with a smile. "And business?"

"Booming!" exclaimed David. "As you know, the south side has exploded, and the city just keeps growing." He went on with details of some recent transactions until he noticed soft snoring and that his uncle's head had dropped onto his chest. David quietly pushed the wheelchair back to his uncle's room. He steered his car back to the city and his empty suite at the Palmer House.

The Wren

A puddle had formed in the depression at the foot of the park bench where Etta and David had sat chatting forty years before. Gently bobbing on it lay a lone pine needle. The park welcomed the spring of 1920, and fragrant blossoms added even more ambiance to the fresh air.

A lone, tiny brown wren landed on the bench, then hopped down to the puddle. Snatching up the pine needle, she flew back up into the tree and, head bobbing, wove it carefully into her nest.

She threw back her head, opened her beak, and trilled a song straight from a heavenly realm.

The End

(Thank you for leaving a review)

Epilogue

Transcription of actual letter sent by Etta's granddaughter, little Henrietta*, age 13, sent from Chicago on July 3rd, 1917 to her mother, Claire. (Copied exactly as written.)

"Dear Mother, I got here alright and grandady and Marion met me at the depot. We rode home in a limousine. We went home on the lake shore drive. Today we went shopping and got the birds some things. I saw some gunea pigs and little bit of poodle dogs and a hundred dollar parrot that talked. I have been reading some interesting dog stories and I am waiting for dark so we can go down to the lake and see the lights. We are going to the Majestic theater Thursday. I have been sleeping on a porch. Lovingly, Henrietta"

*(name changed)

Made in the USA
Middletown, DE
25 October 2023